Living. With ghosts.

LINX & BOGIE

Linx Maxwell's life is on the verge of greatne s. She's finally graduated from street fairs and hopping cha n link to making art that pays the bills. Her family life is… not dull. And it looks like her van might just be able to exist n hope and duct tape.

If only she could get rid of the ghost who's plagued her since the eighth grade.

Frank Bogle is a detective who lost his life in the line of duty. Everyone on the other side knows that the Maxwell women are the best mediums in the business, but did he have to get attached to the one whose hair had been attacked by a weed-wacker?

Frank doesn't like his afterlife any more than Linx does. He just doesn't know how to leave.

LINX & BOGIE is a short fiction, paranormal series by Elizabeth Hunter, author of the Elemental World, the Irin Chronicles, and the Cambio Springs Mysteries.

A GHOST IN THE GLAMOUR

A Linx & Bogie Mystery

ELIZABETH HUNTER

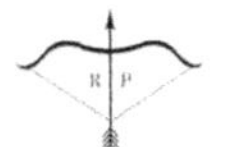

Recurve Press, LLC
PO Box 4034
Visalia, CA 93278
USA

Morning Cupcake

2002

IT WAS the smell of cigarette smoke that woke me that morning. I twitched my nose and stretched out my legs before I rolled over and into the beam of morning sun that came through my window. I could feel the sheets covering my legs ripple in the breeze my window caught. The scent of Venice Beach in the morning drifted through my window. Salt and coffee. A little trash.

And cigarette smoke.

That smell hadn't been in my nan's house since my grandfather had died when I was ten. Three years later, it still reminded me of him.

"Morning, cupcake," a gravelly voice said.

I rolled over with wide eyes.

And I screamed.

I screamed bloody murder.

"Oh for…" The ghost winced. "Will you quiet down,

kid? If I wasn't dead, you'd have ruptured my eardrums." He pinched the bridge of his nose.

"MO-OOM!" I scrambled to the corner of my bed, my head resting against the giant orange star I'd painted on the wall. "NANA!" I pulled the sheets up to my chin.

I heard frantic steps pounding up the stairs.

"Lins?"

"*Lindsay?*"

Both my grandmother and mother were shouting my name, but I was frozen, staring at the ghost. I don't know why I was so shocked. I was thirteen. I'd hit puberty the year before and, to be completely honest, a ghostly visit was overdue. (Kind of like my boobs. I was still waiting for those.) But the ghost thing… My mom and nan had begun glancing at me with concern when they thought I wasn't looking.

Surely, Lindsay wouldn't be the first Maxwell woman in four hundred years—

"Who is it?" The door burst open. My mom came right to me, no doubt suspecting the reason for my panic. "Lindsay, baby, calm down."

I was shaking my head back and forth, my mouth shut and my eyes like saucers.

Nan stood in the doorway. "Well, it's about time. I'm sorry you've had a shock, luv, but there you go. First visit all over and I'm sure you'll be able to—"

"He's still here!" I pointed at the corner where the strangely corporeal spirit was. I knew he was a ghost. Why? He had that tiny bit of halo around him. Not the kind of halo you're thinking of. Trust me, this ghost didn't look like an angel, but that little glow around the apparition did let me know the creepy old guy sitting in the corner of my room wasn't human, which meant he couldn't hurt me.

"Oh?" Nan was surprised. "Well, that's considerate."

"*Why?*" I shouted. "How is that considerate?"

"He could have just flitted in the room and out again," Nan said.

"Or done the weird peripheral vision thing," Mom added.

Nan shuddered. "I hate that. My first spirit played around for weeks. I thought I'd go mad."

I groaned and hid my face. Why me? Why did I have to be born into a family of freaks?

My mom stroked my hair. "Lins, calm down. We're Maxwells. We are not afraid of ghosts."

The old guy was just sitting in the corner, his legs stretched out, his thumb tapping on the edge of the purple painted armchair he was sitting in. He looked like he belonged in a black and white movie, complete with slicked-back hair, suit and tie. He was even wearing one of those old-fashioned hats. Not a top-hat. I think they called it a fedora or something.

The ghost sighed and looked around my room. "Trust me, kid, I'm not any happier about this than you are."

His clear disapproval of my obviously awesome living quarters made me sneer. It also calmed me down, which was good, I guess.

"Are you okay?" my mom asked.

"Yes." And kind of annoyed with Judgey, the Not-Friendly Ghost over in the corner.

"Good." My mom took a deep breath. "Now, have you greeted the spirit?"

I shook my head.

"Lindsay, that's not acceptable. Just because someone is dead doesn't mean they don't deserve the same level of courtesy—"

"Hey!" I pointed at the corner. "He called me 'cupcake,' so why don't you give him the lecture? Is that polite?"

My mom and nan's eyes both swung toward the corner, and even though I knew they couldn't see the ghost, they narrowed their eyes.

"Besides, Mom, if you woke up with a weird guy in your room—"

"Cut that out, will ya? I'm not some pervert." The ghost scowled. "You think I got any control over this mess?"

I glared. "Why are you even here?"

"Lindsay Evelyn Maxwell," my nan warned.

"Manners, Lins."

I ignored them both, which was… not unusual.

"And don't call me 'cupcake' again." I pointed my finger. "Do I look like a cupcake?"

He scoffed. "You look like a twelve-year-old boy. Who cut your hair? The lawnmower?"

I scrambled toward him and off my bed with a raised fist only to collide with the purple chair in the corner. I whirled around and he was leaning against the door to my bathroom.

"Listen, kid—"

"Shut up! You are a big, giant… jerk! And I want you

out of my room. Now!" I crossed my arms over my nonexistent boobs, still self conscious about being in my pjs in front of a strange man, even if he was a ghost.

To other people, I may have seemed like the quiet artsy girl who hovered on the edge, but in my family, I knew how to make my voice heard. I had to. Respect for personal space was not a Maxwell Family Value.

Everyone waited, but the spirit made no move to leave or… disappear. Dissolve. Whatever he did. I wasn't sure quite what to expect.

"Is he… still here?" Mom asked.

"Yes." I glared at him. "I don't want a creepy old man in my room right now. Or ever."

"Hey!" He put his hands on his fists. "Don't call me creepy. And I'm not that old. It's not like I knew my medium was going to be a pipsqueak kid."

"I am *thirteen*, dude, and you are *so* old. I think my grandpa had a suit like that. Plus you smell like cigarette smoke, which is just gross. I'm not the one with bad manners here. Get out of my room. You don't have permission to wake me up like that. *Ever.* If you need to tell me something, find me when I'm in the kitchen or something. Being in my room is *so not cool.*"

I saw him sneer and mouth the words 'so not cool,' but I didn't budge. I could feel my nan and mom behind me, listening to my one-sided conversation. They didn't speak, and I was relieved. This may have been my first ghost, but I knew I needed to deal with him.

"I mean it," I said. "You want me to shut the door on you?"

His eyes narrowed. "You can't do that."

"Not yet," I admitted. "But she can." I pointed to my mom. "And she can too." I pointed to my nan. "You want my first lesson of the day to be how to banish a ghost? Because I'm sure they'd be happy to teach me."

Old Guy just glared at me some more. The scent of tobacco grew stronger, and I knew he was mad.

"I'm a Maxwell," I said calmly. "I know how this works, and I know I may be the only chance you get. So what's it going to be, dude?"

Boundaries. If I'd heard the lecture once, I'd heard it a thousand times. You had to have strict boundaries with spirits. Maxwell women were powerful mediums, but give a ghost an inch and they would take a mile. They'd take over your life if you weren't strong enough. Haunt your days and nights. Never let you have the semblance of a normal life. Even drive you crazy.

There were plenty of stories about that.

Boundaries.

Old Guy and I glared at each other for what felt like ages. He finally let out a frustrated breath and said, "Fine. But please, stop calling me dude. I *hate* that word."

"Okay." Massive relief I tried not to show. "So who are you?"

"The name's Frank Bogle." He started to put his hand out, then drew it back and stuck both hands in his pockets like he didn't know what to do with them. "Detective, LAPD."

I tried to think of any titles I had. *Lindsay Maxwell, Art Achievement Award, Mark Twain Middle School?*

"Nice to meet you, Frank. I'm Linx."

"Your mom and grandmother called you Lindsay."

"Yes, but my friends call me Linx, and I prefer that."

"Cupcake—" he started to fade away in front of me. "—let's make one thing clear: I may talk to you, but I am *not* your friend."

2016

I WOKE SMELLING CIGARETTE SMOKE. It could have been my neighbors, but the new couple living next door were tech people playing at the bohemian, artistic life in newly revitalized Venice Beach, which meant there was usually some weed mixed in with the tobacco when it was my neighbors.

Which could only mean—

"Morning, Cupcake."

I groaned and rolled over, flipping Frank the bird over my shoulder while I tried to hide under the covers.

It didn't matter. After fourteen years with the stubborn jackass, I knew he wouldn't go away.

"Let's go, kid. We got a job."

YOU CAN DO THIS, Linx. You can *do this.*

I was here. It was finally happening. My worst nightmare.

High school.

A giant knot sat in the pit of my stomach and a ghost hung over my shoulder.

"Why are you even here?" I hissed.

"What else am I supposed to do?" Frank asked.

"Oh, I don't know. Leave me to suffer alone?"

"Why would I do that?"

Tears threatened at the corner of my eyes. I was such a freak. People who thought I could start over were kidding themselves. Venice Beach wasn't that big a town. The people who called me a freak in middle school were still here, haunting my steps more effectively than Frank. And he was my actual ghost.

You can do this, Linx.

No, you can't. You're an idiot and everyone is going to find out who you are.

Isn't there something called home study I could be doing right now?

The last six months of eighth grade, the bullying at my last school had gotten so bad, my mom pulled me out and let me stay home to finish my classes. I'd aced them. School had never been that hard. Putting up with the taunts of "Ghost Girl" and "freak" were much harder.

But then Nan decided I needed to give high school a try. There were art classes I couldn't take at home, she said. It was a new place with new people, she said.

Okay, I said.

The hope had lasted until a week before classes started. Then the terror set in.

I could pretend I was leaving "Ghost Girl" behind, but eventually, I was going to have to abandon the sidewalk and enter the high school so I could find my first period class. When I did that, someone was going to recognize me, or see me muttering to Frank, or I'd drop my sketch-book, or *something*.

It would all be over, and I'd be the freak again.

"Kid, you gotta shake it off," Frank said. "You're panicking. Panicking never got anyone anywhere. You're Lindsay Maxwell—"

"Linx."

Frank sighed. "What is wrong with Lindsay?"

"Linx is cooler. It sounds like an artist."

"Okay."

He was humoring me. I hated that more than anything.

"Frank, of all the days for you to pretend I don't exist, this would be a good one to pick. Just… go away."

"Sorry, cupcake. For some reason, I get the feeling I need to stick by you today."

"Ignore that feeling!" I readjusted my backpack and prepared to walk up the path. "And leave me alone. Just… leave me alone. Just for today, okay? Just for today, let me pretend that I'm normal. That I'm just an ordinary girl."

"God's sakes, kid. *Just* relax, will ya? Why do you want to be normal anyway? Normal people are boring as hell. Pardon my language, but it's true."

I didn't tell Frank, but it gave me a little thrill anytime he cursed in front of me. My mom and my nan would be appalled, but then they were pretty appalled that the ghost of a grown man was stuck to their fourteen year old daughter and granddaughter. Their horror at the situation was the only thing that made it bearable most days.

Because most days, I wanted to murder Bogie.

If he wasn't already dead.

"Okay." I took a deep breath. "Here I go."

"You're gonna be great, kid."

"Shut up, Frank."

Two boys pushed past me, looked over their shoulders, and smiled.

"Who's she talking to?" one asked.

"A ghost, I guess."

They burst into laughter. I wanted to sink into the ground.

Then I saw Bogie on the path ahead, walking back and forth through the boys who'd teased me, his presence making them so uncomfortable they looked like they were about to puke.

Okay, maybe having Frank here wouldn't be *all* bad.

"Thanks," I said quietly when I felt him return to my side.

"No problem."

———

"LINDSAY MAXWELL?" the teacher called.

"Linx," I answered. "Just Linx." For the fourth time that day.

She was young and seemed cool. She made a note on the board in her hand and continued with the roll call. So far, I'd been able to escape any kind of attention. I didn't care about making friends. It probably sounded lame, but I didn't need friends. I had my mom and my nan. I had Bogie. I just didn't want to become a target again.

I was in fourth period, a French class I was pretty excited about, and I'd been assigned my favorite seat. Back of the class in the corner. Bogie was leaning against the back wall, checking out my teacher with a little smile on his face. I shot him a dirty look over my shoulder and heard a muffled laugh from my left.

I turned and saw a boy. A beautiful boy. He had skin the color of raw umber, green-hazel eyes, and the longest eyelashes I'd ever seen. His lips looked like a supermodel's, and I could feel myself blushing bright red. I quickly looked down at my desk and pretended to ignore him.

A note hit my shoulder. I unfolded it and read: *What did the cabinets do to you?*

I looked over at him. He'd seen me glaring at Bogie. I just shook my head and went back to doodling on the edge of my notebook.

Another note hit my shoulder. I looked up with wide eyes.

Beautiful boys didn't pay attention to me. I was skinny and I wore black all the time so if I got paint on my clothes, they wouldn't stain. Beautiful boys paid attention to girls with boobs, which I didn't have. Was this guy messing with me? Why? What had I done to him.

He didn't look mean, though. His eyes were kind when he nodded at the note he'd tossed me.

I like your name, it said.

I angled my notebook toward him. *Thanks.*

He angled his notebook toward me. *I'm Raul. You were staring at your thumb when she called my name.*

I remembered his name, I just hadn't been paying attention to his face. Or to anyone's faces.

Your last name is French, I wrote. *Are you French?*

Haitian. But I speak French.

So why are you in this class?

Easy A.

I smiled. If I could get an A in Supernatural Communication, I'd take it. *Maybe you can check my homework. I suck at everything but art.* It wasn't precisely true, but it felt like it most days.

I've never seen doodling that good. He nodded at my notebook. *That's amazing.*

No other compliment could have made me like him more. *Thanks.*

We had to pay attention after that. Our teacher, Mademoiselle Gerard, was passing out textbooks and explaining the syllabus. The hour flew by, and by the time we were packing up, French had gone to the top of my preferred classes, right under Art. If nothing else, I could take mental pictures of Raul to sketch later when he couldn't see.

"Hey," he said after the bell had rung.

"Ohmygosh, your voice is really nice too," I said in a rush.

Raul laughed, but it was true. His voice had definitely dropped early. There was none of the crackling most of the boys my age had.

I turned bright red again. "Sorry."

"Hey Linx."

"Yeah?"

"If I tell you a secret, you'll stop blushing."

"I really doubt that," I muttered, hoisting my backpack on my shoulder.

Raul leaned in—*ohmygoshhesmelledsogood*—and whispered, "Girls aren't really my type." He pulled back, winked, and stretched his arms out. "I have lunch now. You want to eat with me?"

Oh. *Oh!*

But he was kidding if he thought I was going to stop blushing. He was still way too handsome not to embarrass me.

Wait, had he invited me to eat with him?

I asked, "Don't you already have friends here?"

He shook his head. "No one with a cool name and insane artistic talent. You?"

"I was homeschooled most of last year," I said quietly. "Cause… people kinda suck."

A flash of understanding in his eyes. "Yeah."

"But I'd love to sit with you for lunch. If you're inviting me."

"Cool." He walked out of the classroom and I followed. "Buying or bagging?"

"Bagging. My nan—my grandma—thinks the food the school serves is made of poison and plastic."

Raul laughed. "She sounds like my grandma."

Bogie followed us down the hall, hovering over my shoulder.

"He's is a good one, kid," Bogie said quietly. "He's the kind worth knowing."

Yeah. I smiled. I had a feeling Bogie was right.

———

FRANK WATCHED Linx with her new friend, grateful for the kindness he saw in the boy's eyes. Frank watched them sit under a tree, chatting away, grateful she'd found someone she liked.

High schools were so damn big now. When he'd been in school, he knew everyone in his class. He didn't know how that was possible at a big city school like this one. It looked more like a college campus to him, except high school kids were still little shits.

Linx attracted more attention than she realized. When she grew into her face and got more confident, she was going to be a looker. Those boys harassing her that morning weren't just teasing her. He'd caught them giving her the eye, but not in the innocent way Raul was looking. He'd felt the oily darkness around them, and he was keeping his eyes open.

Linx might think he was a hardass, but he worried about her. The last year at her middle school had been hell. Sometimes, he suspected Linx left her room just so she could give him shit about following her. It was the only thing she seemed to enjoy about her life. That and her drawing. He was grateful when Peggy had convinced her mom to let her study at home.

It wasn't like Frank didn't know his little medium was in for a rough time being stuck with him. He tried to give her as much privacy as possible, but other than a few nudges he got from passing spirits, Linx's life was his life. He was stuck with her the same way she was stuck with him.

Linx was his now, whether she wanted it or not.

Frank kept his distance in the shaded courtyard, keeping watch over Linx and Raul as they got to know each other. The new boy was smart enough to keep her interested, perceptive enough to realize Linx wasn't like other girls, and confident enough that he didn't make himself a target. Frank approved.

He saw the two boys from earlier in the day spot Linx with Raul. Their lips curled, and Frank drifted over to listen in.

"—Ghost girl. I heard about her. She has like… serious problems."

"Mental problems?" the other boy asked.

"Something." The first boy nodded at Linx and Raul. "Looks like she found another freak like herself."

Both boys looked like the stereotypical "cool kids" Frank had become accustomed to seeing in Southern California. Both were Caucasian with blond tipped hair that might have been from the sun or a bottle. He couldn't tell the difference. They had deep tans and spiked hair. Their t-shirts had the name of a surfboard brand on them and looked pressed.

Spoiled rich kids, Frank thought. Interchangeable and boring. Nothing nearly as interesting as an anti-social little artist with acidic humor who drank her coffee black. These two didn't deserve to breath the same air as his girl. He could feel his irritation turning darker.

"I don't even get why freaks like them are allowed in school," the second boy said. "Shouldn't they have, like separate schools for freaks?"

Both boys laughed.

"Shouldn't they have separate schools for idiots?" Frank muttered.

"I wonder if I have any classes with her," the first boy asked. His eyes were gleaming and Frank caught the scent of a predator.

This one could be dangerous.

"Not likely. She's a freshman, dude."

"Maybe I'll find a way to get to know her." He sneered. "Give her a proper welcome to high school."

The burst of rage was quick and enervating. Frank took advantage of it, shoving his hand on the back of the boy's head, pushing his face into the tray of spaghetti on the table.

"What the fuck?" the punk sputtered as he wiped his face and stood. "Who did that?"

Frank checked Linx, but she was all the way across the courtyard. She hadn't even noticed the boy. The punk was standing with red sauce on his face, glaring at all the kids laughing around him.

"Hey, Jordan," one girl said. "I think you have a little something on your face."

She had a coterie of girls around her, all giggling at the boy named Jordan.

"Something on my face? Isn't that what I told you last night, Ashlee?"

If looks could kill…

Frank drifted away from the drama at the lunch tables, satisfied that the boy's attention had been averted. No one was looking at Linx. All the attention seemed to be toward the kids at the lunch tables.

Still, Frank would make a note to keep an eye on that Jordan kid. Bullies didn't care if they picked good targets for their rage. They just picked easy ones.

Far off on the grass, Linx laughed at something Raul said, and the sound lifted the dark cloud Frank had been under all day.

Remember, kid, you don't need a lot of friends. You just need one if they're good.

———

LUNCH WITH RAUL was so much better than I ever could have guessed. Raul was awesome and funny and everyone ignored us, except some of the girls who were checking him out when they thought he didn't notice. Raul noticed, by the way. Every single one of them. He noticed everything, but… he actually seemed to like me. Plus, he was great at giving tips about who to avoid and how to fly under the radar with the older kids.

By the time I headed to Art, my last class of the day, I was hopeful I'd be able to avoid the stigma of junior high. I figured, if I could get through the first week of high school without attracting any attention, people would leave me alone for the year. They'd have their little groups, and I'd be safe.

I'd made it to the classroom. I could smell the paint and lingering scent of turpentine. I was almost home…

"Ghost Girl!" a voice said behind me.

My stomach dropped. I didn't want to turn, but I couldn't stop myself.

It was the boy from this morning, but he was wearing a different shirt. He looked older than me, and much bigger. I ignored him and practically ran into the classroom, Bogie at my heels. I could feel his aura, all spiky and dark, but he couldn't do anything. It took a lot of energy for a spirit to affect anything in the physical world.

"Ignore him," Frank said. "Get into class. Go introduce yourself to the teacher."

Yeah, cause that didn't sound dorky at all.

"Ghost Girl!" the older boy called again, the sick laughter was all for my benefit. He knew he was getting to me.

I walked to the front of the empty classroom to see a Latino man with a grey ponytail making marks in his book. He looked up over half-moon glasses, and his dark brown eyes met my panicked ones.

"Can I help you?" he asked slowly.

I'd purposely rushed to Art. I wanted to get the best table if I could. I was the only one there. Me… and my new tormenter.

"Hi. My name is Linx—Lindsay Maxwell, and I'm in this class and I just wanted to know if I could get a seat by the window because I love natural light when I'm painting and also I love art." I blinked hard, praying that I wouldn't cry.

I'd almost made it. This morning when I woke up, I knew two things: I would make no friends in high school, and art class would be my sanctuary. It was the one thing about high school that I was really excited about. The whole reason I was here.

It looked like I might have been wrong on both points. I *think* I had a new friend in Raul, and art class might just be the worst.

The boy hadn't left the classroom. He was standing behind me, excited by my fear. I could feel him feeding on it like a parasite.

The teacher looked at me, then looked at the boy behind me. "Can I help you?" he asked the boy.

"Yeah, I'm in this class too. Can I sit by her?"

No no no no no.

The teacher looked back at me and I tried to communicate how much I did *not* want this guy anywhere near me. I could feel Bogie walking back and forth through the kid, trying to throw him off. It wasn't working. The boy was too excited by my discomfort.

"You look a little old to be in beginning art," the teacher said. "What year are you?"

"Junior," the boy said. "But I'm behind on my fine art requirement."

"And what's your name?"

"Jordan Kinsecki."

"Hmmm." He scratched his pencil on his temple as he looked at his book. "Well, I'm Mr. Rivera. And I'm afraid I don't have you on my roll, Jordan."

"I'm transferring into this class," Jordan said.

I bet you are, asshole.

"You already talk to your counselor about that?" Mr. Rivera said.

"I will."

"I'm not sure we'll have room." The teacher met my eyes, and in that moment, I knew I had an ally. "You'll have to get approval from me and your counselor."

"I told you. I need it."

"Talk to your counselor then," he said. "For now, you can take the front corner desk. I don't have time to deal with this right now, Mr. Kinsecki. Sort your schedule out with your counselor after school, then come talk to me."

The boy didn't leave. I could feel him hovering at my back.

The teacher cocked his head. "Didn't I tell you to take your seat?"

"Yeah." I felt him retreat.

I stood in front of the art teacher, shoulders slumped. I could see his seating chart. He had plenty of spaces. Jordan Kinsecki was going to make it into the class if he wanted it. I'd be dealing with him all year in the one place I'd hoped would be my refuge.

"Hi," the teacher said. "Like I said, I'm Mr. Rivera. Linx is a cool name. Do you prefer that to Lindsay?"

"Yes, please."

"I believe you're on the third row back closest to the windows, Linx."

"Good light," I said. It was hard not to feel defeated, even though I was thrilled to be closest to the windows.

"It's a good seat." Mr. Rivera said. He dropped his voice. "Do you have a problem with that young man?"

How much to tell? What to tell? I didn't want to be the complaining girl. The girl who cried bully. Complaining about the harassment at my middle school had done nothing but make it worse.

"I don't know him," I said.

"That's not what I asked."

Bogie said, "Tell him. Tell him, Linx. This guy gets it."

I took a deep breath. "I don't know him. But he's going to call me Ghost Girl all year. He knows… someone. He heard about me from someone."

"Ghost Girl?"

"Yeah." I left my expression blank. I could feel Frank behind me. I felt the brush of his arm on my neck. It was the closest he got to a hug, and I don't think he realized he did it.

"So…" Mr. Rivera steepled his fingers. "Do you see ghosts?"

I didn't say anything, figuring it wasn't a serious question. Of course I didn't see ghosts. Only crazy people saw ghosts, right?

Frank said, "Tell him, kid."

"Don't want to," I said under my breath.

"Well no," Mr. Rivera said. "I suppose seeing spirits would be upsetting for most people. The fact that you do means you must have a very strong personality and sense of self."

Wait… did he believe me? I frowned.

"I'll keep an eye on Mr. Kinsecki," he said. "But keeping him from taking the class might cause more trouble than it's worth. Do you understand?"

I understood I had a kickass teacher. "Yeah," I said. "I get what you mean."

Mr. Rivera smiled as the other students started to mill about the classroom. "So you like art?"

"I love art." I smiled too. "When I grow up, I'm going to be an artist."

Mr. Rivera stood and leaned toward me. "Something tells me you already are."

I walked to my desk, and Jordan Kinsecki was the last thing on my mind. I glanced around the classroom and saw a couple of girls standing at the back, worn sketchbooks in hand, surveying the classroom from the edges. I saw a guy with black hair hanging in his eyes, sitting at a desk and staring down at the paper where he was drawing a skateboard. Mr. Rivera was talking to another boy in the front, and I noticed his shirt had green paint on the hem.

And there was Jordan Kinsecki, awkwardly sprawled in the desk in the darkest corner, his overly styled hair and brand-name t-shirt standing out like a sore thumb.

"See, kid," Frank said. "In this place, he's the freak."

"Looks like it."

"He might hang around anyway."

I glanced at Frank from the corner of my eye. "Maybe

it wouldn't be so bad for you to come to class with me. If you want to."

He sat in the empty chair beside me. "I got nothing better to do." He stretched transparent legs and crossed them at the ankles. "Besides, that Mademoiselle Gerard is some dame."

I rolled my eyes. "Oh my gosh, Bogie, don't be gross. She's my teacher."

He smiled and faded away just as the boy with paint on his shirt sat in the chair he'd been occupying.

"Hey," the boy said.

"Hey." I looked at his hands. They had paint on them too, so I stuck out my hand. "My name is Linx."

"NOW, you're going to ease off the brake," Nan said, "and press down on the gas."

The slow roll made my heart pound when my foot left the brake. I pressed down ever so slightly…

The car jerked forward and I slammed my foot back on the brake.

"Jeez, kid! It's a good thing ghosts can't get whiplash," Frank said from the backseat. "But think of your grandmother, will ya?"

"Frank," Nan said. "You need to calm down. I can feel your energy from up here, even though I can't hear you."

I kept my foot planted firmly on the brake. "This is not a good idea."

"You have to learn how to drive, Lindsay. You live in Los Angeles."

"I'll make Raul drive me!" He already had his license and the keys to his grandma's old Buick.

"That is not a reasonable long term plan," Nan said.

"You need to learn how to drive. Now take your foot off the brake and try again."

Had my mom's old Honda always been so huge? I used to think the Civic was cramped, but somehow, in that deserted Sears parking lot, it seemed massive. I slowly took my foot off the brake and rolled forward.

"Now press the gas."

"Slowly," Frank said.

"Do you have to be here?" I asked. "Don't you have… ghost things to do?"

Nan said, "Oh Lindsay, darling, don't be rude. Frank is part of the family. It's Christmas."

"You're a treasure, Peggy."

"You always say that," I muttered.

"Who are you talking to?" Nan asked.

"Both of you! You're both here to torment me." The car was rolling forward and my foot was hovering over the gas pedal. I had a vision of my foot pressing down and the car rocketing into the front of Sears where a row of giant concrete pylons sat. Probably to keep the front of the store safe from teenage drivers.

"I can't do this."

"You can do this," Nan said.

"I'm already dead," Frank said. "So it doesn't really matter if you kill me."

"Frank!"

I was probably the only sixteen year old in the world who screamed in terror when car keys with a bow on them fell out of my stocking on Christmas morning. Nan had calmed me down and told me I was long overdue. She and my mom couldn't keep driving me around forever. The "Raul has a car" argument fell on deaf ears.

"Lindsay."

"Yes?"

"Lindsay. Dear girl."

"Yeah?"

Frank said, "Put your foot on the gas, kid!"

I put my foot on the gas and the car shot forward, but not as fast as the last time. It was a jerk and then I let up and we slowed to a crawl. I coasted with my foot lightly on the accelerator for the length of the parking lot.

I laughed in relief. "I'm driving!"

"Slower than molasses," Frank muttered.

"Shut up, Bogie."

Nan's voice, as always, was the voice of reason. "You're doing very well. But you may want to speed up. Just a little."

"Why?"

"How fast are you going?"

I forced my eyes down to the speedometer and saw the arm pointing at 15mph.

"Okay." I pushed down ever so slightly and the arm pointed to the 20. Then the 25. "Look!"

"Yes, very good," Nan said. "Now, we're coming to the end of a row. You're going to want to slow down a bit and turn right to go around that curb."

Oh no oh no oh no oh no.

I turned the wheel right…

And struck the curb. The jolt threw both of us forward.

"Nan, are you okay?" Oh shit. I probably killed my

grandmother on my first day driving. Not only would I never get a driver's license, my mother was going to ground me forever. I glanced over at Nan after planting my foot firmly on the break again. "Nan?"

"I'm fine." She looked up and I could see she was trying to hold in a laugh. "You're fine. Just put the car in reverse and back up a little."

"How do I do that?"

"You already know, Lindsay."

Did I? I had studied the book endlessly, but in the moment, all I could remember was that it was illegal for women in California to drive in a house coat. That was it. It was the sum totally of my driving knowledge and it had come from a weird email forward Raul had sent me when I turned sixteen.

What was a house coat anyway? What made them so dangerous on the road?

"Okay okay okay." I put my hand down and slid the car into reverse.

"Now take your foot off the brake and—"

"Put it on the gas," I said. "I know."

"No—"

The car shot back and rolled right over a concrete parking stop with my back wheel. I hit the brakes.

Bogie started to laugh.

"Shut up, Frank!"

"Cupcake, you have a ways to go."

I was nearly in tears. Why was this so hard?

"Nan—"

"Lindsay, you need to calm down." Gran pulled out a small flask and took a sip.

My eyes went wide. "Nan, you cannot give me whisky when I am driving, what are you thinking?"

She said, "It's not for you. It's for me. Now, drive forward slowly but firmly. You're going to have to roll over that block again."

I winced every moment, thinking about what I was probably doing to my car, but I managed to roll over the curb and sloooooowly take the right turn at the end of the lane. Just as we were headed back to the far end of the parking lot, I saw another car pull into the driveway.

"We're going to die!" I yelled. "Nan, they can't be here, this is our parking lot! I'm going to run into them and we're all going to die!"

She closed her eyes and took a deep breath. "Calm down."

"I can't!"

"For pete's sake, kid. You're making this twice as hard as it needs to be," Frank said. "Just stop the car and wait for them to pass."

"Okay!"

I stopped the car. I waited. They passed.

And no one died.

"Now pull forward and keep going," Frank continued. "Try a left turn when we get to the end."

"Stop bossing me around," I said. "You're not teaching me to drive."

"Well…" Nan said, sipping another nip of whisky. "That's not a bad idea."

"What's not a bad idea?"

"Frank teaching you to drive," Nan said.

"He can't teach me to drive," I said. "He's a ghost."

"Which means he's probably more relaxed than I am about the whole business." She raised the flask. "You've driven me to drink."

"Yeah, Nan." I rolled my eyes. "It sure takes a lot to drive you into that whisky bottle."

"Mind your manners," she said. "Frank, you go on. She seems to be much more relaxed when she's sniping at you."

"You heard her, kid. You're working for me now."

"What?" I glanced in the rearview mirror. "That is not what she said."

"Watch the stop sign. It's getting close."

I stopped. "The rules are probably totally different than when you were driving, Frank."

"Not that different. Now take a right."

I finally noticed where he'd been guiding me. "What? I can't go on the street! There are other cars out there."

Nan raised her flask. "Well, I can't be driving us home now. You're going to have to step up, dear."

"Don't wave that flask around!" I tried to throw her sweater over the silver flask. "Oh my gosh, Nan, I'm going to get a DUI before I even have my license."

"I don't think they can do that if you're not drinking, kid." He leaned forward and popped his slightly transparent head between the seats. "Okay, there's no one coming. In fact, there's no one on the roads right now, Linx. You're fine. You were driving around the parking lot just fine."

"Because there were no other cars!"

"Turn right," he said calmly. "And stay in the middle lane."

Trembling, I pulled forward. Frank was right. There were no other cars on the road. It was Christmas afternoon. Everyone in town was sitting at home eating or napping or playing with presents or doing something other than driving, because it was the most deserted I'd ever seen it. I stayed in the middle lane for four blocks.

"Now you're gonna take a left, kid."

Convinced I was going to die, I moved to the left turn lane and paused. There was a car coming in the distance.

"What are you doing?" Frank asked.

"Waiting for that car."

"That car must be five blocks away."

"So?" I asked. "Better safe than sorry."

"There's a stop-sign on every block!"

"Calm down, Frank." I smiled. "It seems like you're getting tense. You don't want to be tense while I'm driving, do you?"

"Are you joshing me, kid?"

"I don't even know what that means." The car finally passed. There was another one coming, but there was also someone waiting behind me at this point. I didn't want to be a jerk. I pulled forward and got in the center lane.

"Get in the right lane," Frank said.

"Why?"

"Because you're going to turn right eventually."

"Define eventually."

Nan opened her eyes. I think she'd taken a little nap with all the whisky she'd drunk so far. She wasn't an alcoholic, but on Christmas… she did her ancestors proud. At least, that's the way she put it.

"Where are we?" she asked.

"I have no idea," I said. "Ask Frank."

"We're taking the scenic route, Peggy. The *slow* scenic route. We're traveling in time, in fact. Backward."

I smiled at Nan. "He says we're almost home."

"That's not what I said!"

I was starting to get the hang of this thing. It wasn't really all that hard. As soon as I got the acceleration figured out, it was pretty easy. Well, starting and stopping where still a little jerky, but I figured that wasn't too bad. I stopped well behind the white line at every stop sign.

Well. Behind.

"You are not even up to the intersection," Frank said. "Why are you stopping this far back?"

"Just being cautious."

"You're not being cautious, you're being a wimp."

"Nan, Frank is calling me a wimp for not driving faster."

Nan looked over her shoulder. "Don't encourage the girl to be reckless."

"You may be the only teenager in history to be pulled over by a cop for being too slow," Frank muttered.

"Calm down, Bogie." I had this. I totally had this. Driving was easy. And pissing off Bogie was fun.

Nan took another sip of her whiskey just as we turned south on Ocean Avenue.

"Nan, I really wish you'd put that away."

"Why?"

"I only have my permit, but I'm pretty sure you're not supposed to be drinking in the car with me."

She shrugged. "That's a silly law."

Frank said, "Peggy, I'm going to need you to put the flask away."

"Frank says to put the whisky away, Nan."

She twisted her mouth into a frown, but she closed the flask and dropped it in her purse. "Such a straight arrow, that Detective Bogle."

Frank chuckled, but I kept my eyes on the road. Ocean Avenue was bigger, but it also had more traffic. Nevertheless, I kept in the right lane and cruised slowly south.

Very. Slowly.

I was starting to recognize the streets now. Ocean turned into Nelson that turned into Pacific. Four lanes of slow traffic and one nervous teenage driver. We passed North Venice Boulevard and I tried not to hyperventilate when I moved to the left lane. I knew the roads; they were familiar to my feet, my bike, and my skateboard. But *not* to me in a car.

"You okay here?" Frank checked in.

"Yeah, I'm good."

I waited for the light with bated breath. The nerves were starting to come back. What if I turned into the wrong lane? What if the oncoming traffic didn't stop? What if—

"You think you might learn how to drive faster than a baby stroller one of these days?" Frank asked. "I'm not saying you need to go racing, but something over ten miles an hour might keep you from getting rear-ended."

"Shut up, Frank." The light turned green and with a small jerk, I pulled into the intersection. I ended up in the middle of two lanes, but luckily, I was the only one on the road.

"Right lane," Frank said. "*Right!*"

"I know where I'm going!"

"Do you? I've seen blind camels with a better sense of direction."

"Really? You've seen a blind camel? You haven't left Southern California in sixty-something years, Bogie. There a lot of blind camels around I don't know about?" I turned right onto Eastern Court, which was hardly more than an alley with trash bins and illegally parked cars lining both sides of the road. "Besides, do you really think I need to be racing through here, smartass?"

"Lindsay, watch your language."

"Sorry, Nan."

Frank said, "I think you should have turned right on Mildred, rookie. You're lucky there's not a moving van blocking the road."

I passed the sign for Linnie Canal and stopped, waiting for a little boy and his mom to cross the road.

"Oh really? What's the hurry, Frank? Are you late for a… wait, you're dead. You have no where to go but home with me."

"Lindsay!"

"It's fine, Peggy," Frank said. "At least I'm actually dead. Linx just has a dead social life. Which is sadder."

I curled my lip when the road dead-ended into Court A. I turned right. "I am not apologizing to this jerk. Don't even ask, Nan."

"Don't make me speak to your mother, Lindsay."

"Go ahead and speak to her," I said. "Tell her Frank was the one who—"

"Got us home." Frank poked his head between the

seats as I pulled into the driveway behind my Nan's house. "Merry Christmas, kid. Good driving. Try not to get so stressed out next time, will ya?"

Frank disappeared, leaving me safe in one piece, staring wide-eyed at Nan.

"What?" she asked.

"I did it. I drove us home."

"That wasn't so hard now, was it?"

All I could do was grin.

"Can I get out my flask now?" she asked.

"Can I have a drink?"

"Absolutely not." She opened the door. "That Frank Bogle is such a bad influence on you."

A Ghost in the Glamour

1

Bogie gives me reasons to love
my cell phone

YOU KNOW, there's a lot I don't like about modern life. I hate traffic. (I live in L.A. Of course I hate traffic.) I hate leaf-blowers, even though I can understand their utility. And I hate billboards. Dear God, I hate billboards.

But mobile phones?

You know those really annoying people who walk around with an earpiece in, talking on their phones like the other person is in the room? You think they might be crazy at first glance but no, you see that little white cord or earpiece and suddenly they're just an annoying prick with no regard for anyone's auditory space.

That's me.

"Frank, do you understand that I am working?" I nearly shouted. "I know you think this is one of those things that just-can't-wait, but—"

"Cupcake, if someone is paying you to put that crap on their wall instead of the back alley, far be it from me to interrupt your con."

I could hear the infuriating laughter in his voice. I ignored it and focused on the shading for the mural I was painting in the new coffee shop/wine bar in Culver City. The owner had started renovating the space and uncovered an old brick wall that hadn't ever been painted and just had sheet rock nailed into it. Bless his hipster heart, he didn't paint it, but he did change his design idea. Suddenly the modern art had given way to chic industrial, complete with a faux-graffiti wall opposite the wine racks. I was one of five artists who'd been asked to contribute to the project. It was fun. Our murals overlapped in designed chaos, giving the illusion of a graffitied wall that just happened to attract five amazing artists.

I was the best. Of course.

Frank was still talking. "I heard Mrs. Owens. This vandal is avoiding all the security cameras in the alley, so it's not some bored chucklehead. He hasn't hurt anyone yet, but—"

"Not… listening… to… you," I muttered, using my fingers to smear the edge of one corner. I'd used lacquer, paint, and epoxy—along with old newspaper the construction crew had found in the walls—to create a background for a wall of eyes. Suspicious eyes. Laughing eyes. Seductive eyes. All sorts. Not creepy eyes, no matter what Frank said. It was a portrait gallery. Eyes with hints of faces, but nothing clear. The space let the audience imagine their own face, or someone they loved. It was familiar and mysterious at the same time. Mostly, if it made people look at the wall instead of their cell phone screen, I'd consider it a success.

Frank peered over my shoulder and my neck prickled.

I hated when he got too close, though after fourteen years with the guy, I was kind of used to it.

"I think I remember this story." He pointed at some of the yellowed paper. "Writers' strike, right?" He chuckled. "All those fat studio bosses must have been squirming."

I glanced at the date. "That was in 1960. How do you remember that?"

"Cupcake, I was dead, not deaf." He straightened and glanced at the workers installing cold cases at the end of the counter. "How long is this going to take?"

Frank walked across the room, his hands in his pockets, and deliberately hopped through one of the crew who stopped in his tracks and shook his head, no doubt feeling a prickling sensation envelope his whole body.

Someone walked over your grave.

Doubtful, but you might have just walked through a ghost.

"Will you stop that?" I said, adjusting my earpiece. "So not cool. Let me finish this and then I'll deal with your stuff. I'm almost done."

"Fine."

"Don't pout, Bogie."

I could feel him pouting. I glanced over my shoulder and saw him watching the construction crew, leaning against the old brick wall like he was waiting for a cab. He was such a strong presence, I could barely see the brick.

Frank Bogle was a ghost that appeared in my life when I was thirteen years old. At the time, I thought he was ancient, but as I'd grown older I realized Frank had actually died in the prime of his life. He was probably around thirty-five and he dressed in a grey pin-striped suit, wingtips, and a black fedora. I'd never seen him wear anything else, though my nan says ghosts can change their clothes at will. Most stuck to the familiar, which told me my own personal bogieman had been as fastidious in life as he was in death.

If you're thinking film noir private eye, you'd be almost right. Frank had been police detective. He was still a detective; he just had to work through me.

I am *not* a detective, and I only gave Frank my time when I had it. I'm an artist. A working artist, thank you, which means for the first time in my life I was making most of my money from painting. Mural commissions. Street fairs. Etsy shop. Instagram. Websites. Book covers. Tattoo design. Print-on-demand. I did it all. It was the daily hustle of making money doing the thing I loved, and I wouldn't have traded it for a nine-to-five if you gave me a million bucks.

Okay, maybe a million. You could convince me to dye my hair back to a normal color for a million dollars.

But I didn't think I'd need to. Right now, money was pretty good and the hours didn't suck, which meant Frank had been bugging me.

So yes, I was kind of a detective, but only because he was insufferable otherwise.

"Linx!"

I turned at the sound of Jackson Powers' voice. "Hey, Jackson." I couldn't stop my stupid smile. And it was always the stupid smile.

Dammit, he is not that good-looking. Not that… oh shit, he smiled the big smile. Not the little smirky side smile he does sometimes but the big one. And he was doing it looking at my work.

"This looks amazing." He propped his hands on his hips. "I can't believe you're almost done. Thank you so much for coordinating this. You guys finished so much faster than I imagined."

"Not fast enough," Frank called. "Is this guy for real? And could those pants get any tighter?"

I pretended Frank wasn't there. "I'm just glad you liked everyone's work. We've collaborated on shows and exhibitions, so I knew we'd work well together, but it's always a gamble whether a client is going to be pleased with the overall look."

"I confess, I had my doubts when you started." He looked over at Farah's moody piece in the corner. "But now that everything is finished…"

"It works, doesn't it?" Farah's work was dark, bordering on grotesque, and something you wouldn't normally see in a cafe. But I'd paired him to work with Jonny, whose work had a cartoonish feel that lightened Farah's and forced the audience to think about how light and dark often existed side by side.

Just to be safe, I also put it near the lounge area where people were less likely to have food.

"It really, really does." Jackson took a deep breath and crossed his arms. I tried not to ogle blatantly. He was just so cute. Beardy and tattooed, he screamed "trust fund entrepreneur" but I couldn't help it. He was also really smart and easy to work with.

Maybe too easy, to be honest. I had gone high on my price and he hadn't even bargained.

"This drip," Frank muttered. "I swear to God, kid, you could do so much better."

Still ignoring you, Bogie.

"So," I said, "I should be finished by Wednesday morning at the latest."

"What am I going to do without you?" Jackson smiled.

Was he flirting? Oh shit, I was really bad at flirting.

So I smiled my stupid smile, because of course I did. And I laughed a little and gestured toward the door. "I go to the book store down the street a lot, so if your coffee doesn't suck, I might be back."

His eyebrows went up. "Honest."

"Sorry." I hadn't meant to say that. I mean, don't get me wrong, I was picky about coffee, but that sounded obnoxious. "I'm sure it's going to be great."

"Not that she'll like it, pretty boy. She doesn't like anyone's coffee but her own and her nan's." Frank was standing at the window watching the cars drive past. "Can we finish this up, please?"

I'd kill him. If he wasn't already dead.

Though, he was kind of right about the coffee.

"I better finish this." I gestured to the wall. "Get out of your hair."

"You're always welcome." He smiled. "In the shop. We've got wine as a backup if the coffee sucks." He laughed. "I don't know if you really want to hang out in my hair."

I laughed with him. And yes, I thought about his hair because it was long, but not too long and it was really nice. Kind of wavy. The color of good caramel. Wavy caramel.

"Please, make it stop." Frank mimed banging his head

against the wall. "You'd probably get stuck in his hair with all the junk he puts in it."

"Okay! I'm going to finish. Supposed to help my nan cook dinner tonight. Hoping to leave before three so the traffic…"

Jackson grimaced because he was from Omaha or someplace where they ate a lot of wholesome dairy products—I was just going by his teeth—but he'd learned very quickly about Southern California traffic.

"Right. Bye, Linx." He pointed a thumb over his shoulder. "I better go check with the guys. If you need anything before I leave…"

"I'll make sure I wave before I go," I said. "Later, Jackson."

When I turned around, Frank was leaning against the wet paint. Luckily, none of it was going to get on his impeccable phantom suit.

"Cupcake, this guy's a drip. You'd be bored in two minutes if you weren't so dazzled by his teeth."

I put my earpiece in and picked up the brushes I was using to texture the paint. "Shut up, Bogie."

———

"TELL PEGGY about insulting Jackson's coffee," Frank said, leaning against the counter and peering over my nan's shoulder as she browned the beef for the pie. Frank was the only one who called my nan Peggy since my granddad had died.

"I didn't insult his coffee." I was chopping carrots for the shepherd's pie.

"You insulted your boss's coffee?" Nan said. "In his own coffee shop?"

"One, he's not my boss, he's my client. And two, I didn't insult it!"

"You might as well have," Frank said. "Did you see the look on his face?"

"No—wait, he had a look?"

Nan looked up. "Who had a look?"

"Jackson. Frank said he had a look."

"When?"

"When I insulted his coffee."

"I thought you said you didn't insult his coffee." She looked toward Frank. Even though she couldn't see or hear him, she could feel his presence. "Frank, are you telling tales?"

All the women in my family were mediums, but I was the only one who saw Frank. Nan was a geographic medium. She tended to see ghosts who were bound to familiar places, which meant she saw a variety of dead people throughout her day. Mom was a familiar medium, which meant she spoke to dead people who were still hanging out around their loved ones.

Me? No one knew what I was. Grandma had looked in the journals and apparently no Maxwell woman in the past four hundred years had reported being stuck with one ghost her whole life.

God, please don't let me be stuck with Frank my whole life.

Maxwell women were also very Catholic, which meant I prayed about as often as I talked to ghosts. None of us saw any conflict of interest, but we tried not to think about it too much.

"Peggy, you are a treasure." Frank watched my nan with fond eyes. "They don't make women like you anymore. Wish they did."

"Hey!"

Frank adored my nan, even though he refused to say it. He'd known my grandfather when he'd been alive. And by known, I mean arrested. He'd arrested my granddad.

Nan said, "Well, Frank is a good judge of character. What does Frank think of Jackson?"

"He's a drip," Frank said. "Boring pretty boy."

I shrugged. "He hasn't said much."

Nan's eyes danced. "From the agitation I'm feeling in this room, I say you're lying through your teeth, Lindsay."

"So not cool." Frank mimicked me. "Why don't you tell her how straight-laced he is? Law abiding? No Maxwell woman has ever married a rule-follower. You gonna be the first?"

It was true. Maxwell women married conmen and thieves. Fences and forgers. Nice men—not violent—but not precisely on the bright side of the legal line, if you know what I mean. One Maxwell woman had married a pirate and lived very comfortably as a man for most of her life. A man who was shagging the pirate captain on a very nonjudgmental pirate ship, I guess. Her journals weren't too clear on the details. My granddad had been a very successful pawn broker (and sometimes fence) for most of his life, along with being a dedicated husband, father, and grandfather. My dad was a conman who'd ducked out when I was around four, but still sent my mom and I money and postcards from random places like Singapore and the Maldives.

Jackson Powers, on the other hand, was a boy scout. (Seriously, he'd mentioned that he was in the scouts until high school. I didn't even know you could be in the boy scouts for that long.) Which was a little out of range for my normal type, but I figured I didn't need any extra danger in my life. Not when I had Frank trying to make me into his Girl Friday.

"Frank, don't you think Jackson…" I suddenly missed his presence. "Frank?"

He was gone. He rarely up and left like that. Usually, I had to shove him out the door to get rid of him.

When I was young, my mom had described the door to me. She said all people had it, but most people kept it shut all the time. They didn't even know the door was there. In our family, we had a tendency to leave it open. The trick was, we had to learn when to leave it open a crack and when to slam it shut.

For my mom and my nan, slamming it shut was pretty common. For me, it was harder. Frank had been with me for a long time. Slamming the door shut on him felt rude when he was practically part of the family. So yes, I usually kept the door cracked open, but my bogie was also considerate. One thing about the early twentieth century, it did breed the kind of courtesy you rarely see these days. He didn't intrude on private moments, but when it was just my mom, my nan, and I hanging around, Frank usually joined the party.

Frank disappearing felt wrong.

"Nan, do you feel Frank around?"

She closed her eyes and took a deep breath. "He's in the living room."

I heard the TV as I walked down the hall. The air felt heavy around me, and I knew in a second that something was very wrong.

"Bogie?" I halted in the doorway of the living room, spying Frank with his eyes glued to the television. "What's buzzin', cousin?"

A woman on the news was speaking: "Representatives from the LA County Medical Examiner-Coroner's office say the bones of the woman will be examined for evidence, though it's rare that cases like this are solved so many years after they take place. That said, the presence of a note buried with the victim might give them answers, since apparently it's already given them the woman's identity."

A male voice asked, "Deb, didn't you say that LAPD already had a lead?"

"They do, Ray. Of course, when the note found on a dead body is addressed to a deceased LAPD detective, finding a lead on this kind of cold case isn't quite as difficult as it would be otherwise."

Frank's arms were crossed over his chest and two lines marred his forehead.

The male voice continued: "Just to give you some background if you're new to this story, the bones of a woman who died over sixty years ago were uncovered yesterday afternoon in Griffith Park and have now been transferred to the LA County Medical Examiner's office. Though the body was decomposed, the victim's purse was recovered near the body, miraculously giving the police both her identity and leads to a very old case. Right now, the medical examiner's office is in charge of the remains, but LAPD was quick to issue this statement: 'Nina King was last seen outside her home in Los Angeles on November 19, 1952. She was reported missing by a neighbor. The murder of Nina King now appears to be tied to the disappearance of Los Angeles Police Detective Frank Bogle, who vanished on March 14, 1953, while investigating Miss King's missing person case. All of Detective Bogle's files remain in the archives. The LAPD does not close unsolved cases, and we do not forget our own. We will follow every lead to bring closure to the family of Miss King and to determine what happened to Detective Bogle. We believe that answers in one case could lead to both cases being solved.'"

The station switched to commercial as I stared at Frank, my mouth gaping. He looked up for a heartbeat, and then he was gone.

2

Risking arrest with pretty nerds

FRANK DIDN'T HAVE much as a dead guy. A stellar taste in suits. A relentless sense of justice. And me.

And I had Raul.

"I'm going to get fired, I'm going to get fired, I'm going to get fired," Raul chanted as he let me in the back door of the LA County Medical Examiner-Coroner's main building on Mission. Not the pretty historic building in front, but the one where the bodies were kept.

"You're not going to get fired. We do this every time." I patted Raul's cheek and slipped in the maintenance entrance. "I love you, Raul."

"Not enough to let me see your boobs."

"Don't be gross. Besides you don't even like girls."

He shrugged. "But I like boobs."

Raul had massive shoulders that would have made me swoon (if he was anyone other than Raul) and a body I had painted many times. He was my most frequent nude model. His lips would launch a thousand fantasies if I didn't know him so well.

"So why are you getting fired this time?" I played innocent. "Have you been sexually harassing Eduardo again?"

"He wishes." He put the borrowed uniform coat over my shoulders along with an ID lanyard he borrowed from Janie, one of the other lab techs in his department that looked a little like me without the fuchsia hair. Said fuchsia hair was tucked under a black cap so I didn't glow-in-the-dark. Raul ushered me down a familiar dark hallway. There was nobody in the building except for a few guys on intake and security; the ID was just a precaution.

He said, "I am so going to get fired because this is not like other cases, Linx. Usually, you want to see stuff that nobody pays attention to. But *everyone* is paying attention to glamour girl, okay?"

I felt Frank behind me, and I paid no attention to him. He'd disappeared for three days after he'd seen the news, and I was kind of pissed at him. Usually, he was the one harassing me to ask Raul for a favor, but not this time. This one was all me.

"I love you, Raul."

"Not enough. Not nearly enough."

"I'll let you sleep on my nan's couch if you get fired, go broke, and lose your amazing apartment."

"Thanks, that's comforting."

"I hope you understand I really need to see her. It's important and I wouldn't ask otherwise."

Raul had never asked why I needed him to regularly break the law, but I think he thought I worked for an underground newspaper or blog or something. Maybe he just thought I was a freak. We'd been friends since high school. The fact that he worked at the Medical Examiner's office was just a bonus. We had each other's backs, because in our very homogenous Southern California town, we were both considered "out there." My family saw ghosts, so I was teased as the "ghost girl" all through school. His family was Haitian which meant that no matter how many times he went to mass, kids at school still thought his grandma was a voodoo priestess.

Kids are stupid.

(To be fair, Grann Paulette wore awesome scarves and had the habit of spitting ominous-sounding Haitian phrases at little kids who stared at her too long. She found this hilarious. She and my nan got along well.)

When I'd heard the report on the television, I immediately wanted to read the note they mentioned. Something was eating me, and part of it felt like guilt.

I'd never asked Frank now he died. It always seemed too intrusive.

We spent so much time together we'd developed boundaries about certain things. I didn't ask him about his personal life, but he had endless opinions about mine. He rarely offered commentary on my art, though we often talked about his past cases. He was young enough that I'd always suspected he'd died on the job, but asking the specifics felt morbid in a way I didn't want to examine. Frank was my Bogie. My ghost. Thinking about Frank Bogle, the man, made his life something tragic.

But after the news report, I had to know. I'd already put together a rough idea, but seeing glamour girl and the contents of her purse were something I could only do with Raul's help.

"I don't need to see her bones—"

"Yeah, you do," Frank finally spoke up in a quiet voice.

"—just the artifacts found with her body."

"We need to see the body, kid."

I didn't want to see the body. I hated seeing the bodies.

Raul said, "It's the artifacts that have been the most interesting."

We turned down a hallway and I ignored Frank's huffed breath behind me. Like it or not, I steered this ship, and I didn't want to see the body. I wanted to read the note. I wanted to see what Nina King had carried when she died.

Raul punched in a code that let us into a room with stale air scented with dirt and disinfectant. You might wonder how those scents co-existed. So did I. Nevertheless, there it was. Dirt. Disinfectant.

"There wasn't much. And if she had a suitcase or something, it wasn't with her. Just this stuff." He pointed to a box on the end of one counter. Just an ordinary plastic box like the kind my mom uses to store Christmas supplies. Raul opened it and spread his arm out. "There you go, freak."

"Why would there be a suitcase?"

"Because of the note."

"Okay, I'll bite." I peered inside and the first thing I saw was an old piece of stationery that had been stored in an archival plastic sleeve. The envelope was in a separate sleeve and was addressed to Frank Bogle. No address, just his name. I picked up the envelope and set it on the stainless steel counter before I got out my phone.

"Linx."

"It won't end up online. I promise." I snapped a bunch of pics, making sure to get in close enough that I could read the letter from the photograph. I flipped it over and took pictures of the back and the envelope, too. I could feel Frank behind me, trying to read over my shoulder, so I casually pushed the note farther down the counter so he could see it while I looked at the other contents of Nina King's purse.

A lipstick, the metal case still shiny with a little rust at the seams.

A compact mirror.

A silver cigarette case.

A coin purse.

Two bus tickets too faded to read, though I knew techs might be able to read them from the impressions.

A scarf that looked like it could be silk.

I glanced at the purse encased in a large plastic bag. "This is a nice purse."

"Very nice," Raul said. "It's the only reason this stuff is in such good condition. Vintage Hermés leather. The note was hidden in the lining. Guess whoever killed her didn't think to look there. The purse was wrapped in a raincoat and buried on top of the body. Raincoat protected the purse. Purse protected the contents."

"Even the paper."

"Linen stationery. It's the good stuff."

"This woman had money."

"No, but her boyfriend did." Raul raised his eyebrows. "Read the note, Linx."

Frank was on the other side of the room, staring at the wall. I felt like a horrible voyeur, reading a letter that had been addressed to him while he was in the room, but I couldn't ask Raul the right questions if I didn't.

"I'm sorry," I whispered as I picked it up.

"For what?" Raul asked.

Shit. "I just… feel bad for making you risk your job on something this high profile."

He gave me an incredulous look. "Yeah, right."

"What? I do." I quickly took pictures of everything in the box. Tons of them from every angle I could think of. "Here, I've got pics of everything, okay? I can read the note at home." I started putting everything away, exactly as it had been in the box.

"Linx, are you okay?"

"Yeah, of course." My hand paused over the note, and I saw Frank's head turn toward me. Our eyes met for a moment before I picked it up and placed it carefully back in the evidence box. "I'm fine. I'll just head back home and go over everything there. You're working on this?"

His chest puffed up. "Who's the pollen king, baby?"

He was so pretty, but at the end of the day, he was still such a nerd. A pretty, pretty nerd.

"You are, of course." I patted his cheek. "I'd call you the pollen *god*, actually."

"Now you're just sucking up and it doesn't sound sincere."

I stood on my toes and kissed his cheek. "Thank you. Really, thanks."

"Okay, okay. Don't get mushy." He put the evidence box back on the shelves and nodded toward the door. "When we get back to the maintenance entrance, you can show me your boobs there."

I'd punch his shoulder, but I'm pretty sure I'd only hurt myself.

———

FRANK WAS SITTING SILENTLY next to me in the car. I usually had a good read on his emotions, but that night I was coming up blank. We were stopped at one of those endless red lights on Venice Boulevard, so I picked up my phone and switched to one of his favorite albums.

Duke Ellington and John Coltrane. 1963. One of the best albums *ever*. I had it digital and it was one of the few albums I'd bought on vinyl, too.

Maybe it was inevitable that I'd love jazz growing up with a ghost who defined years by album releases, but I would always appreciate the music Frank had introduced me to. Some of my happiest teenage memories consisted of searching out music online from obscure albums Frank had only heard of. He'd name an album and I'd search for it online as he looked over my shoulder. He thought the internet existed for jazz aficionados.

As the strains of the first track died down, he asked, "Are you going to read it?"

Yes.

"Do you want me to?"

He frowned. "Yes. But in context."

"So tell me the context."

"No."

"Why not?"

His face lost its melancholy and the corners of his mouth turned up. "Because I can show you."

"What—oh Frank! Not that. Can't you just tell me?"

"Nope. It's not the same."

I growled low in my throat. "Fine."

It was something we only did occasionally. My mom was the kind of medium who regularly let spirits sit in the front of her mind and show her stuff. That was because my mother usually only dealt with grief-stricken people who needed to say goodbye to a family member or find out someone's last wishes. She could let a spirit sink deep enough into her mind that she could even take on handwriting and signatures. Trust me, more than one will has been signed by my mother for spirits who were a little late in their estate planning.

She could do that kind of thing because her own talents were incredibly strong.

When Frank sat in my mind to show me memories, I could see a scene from his point-of-view. Which meant I *was* Frank… kind of. It was a little like putting on a suit that was scratchy and didn't fit. Not my favorite thing and it took some kind of focus we could share. Which, for me and Frank, meant that I'd be chain-smoking Lucky Strikes for the duration of the vision.

So. Gross.

We got home and I pulled the dreaded box from the bottom of my desk drawer before I went outside and sat in the back garden. "Okay, this better not take too long. You've only got three left."

The last vision had been over six months ago and I hadn't gotten another pack of cigarettes. I always hoped I wouldn't need them again, but then we'd be working on a case and Frank would stop and say that he couldn't explain something, he needed to show me.

Personally, I think he's just a dirty, dirty nicotine addict.

I grabbed a beer and sat at the picnic table I'd repainted the summer before. Everything in the backyard —fence, furniture, pots and planters—had been painted and repainted by me multiple times. Painting is what I do when I get stressed out.

I struck a match and put a Lucky Strike in my mouth. "Okay, Bogie, hope you're enjoying this."

"Oh yeah, having a punk kid in my head is always a fun experience."

I felt Frank settle behind me as I lit the cigarette. Then he leaned forward and…

3

One of the good boys

FRANK HANDED his fedora to the coat check and glanced at his hair in the mirror before he made his way down the hallway. Medium height. Medium build. A face his mother had loved until she didn't. A face that had cop written all over it.

This club may have been neutral territory for the various criminal organizations in Los Angeles, but that didn't mean a cop was welcome.

He wasn't.

The slow brush of cymbals painted the air as he made his way past the hostess, slipping a ten in her waiting palm before he passed unmolested into the dark club on Central Avenue. His snitch said Mintz's newest girl would be here solo.

And she was.

Tucked into a booth near the back, Nina King's face was illuminated by the cigarette she pulled from a silver case on the table. A quick flare of light, then the booth was bathed in darkness again as the trumpet pleaded for mercy on the stage. The slow piano kept rhythm with Frank's steps as he made his way toward her, following the glowing tip of her cigarette and the smoke the curled around her. He unbuttoned his jacket and slid across from Nina King, ignoring the curl of her lip and the watchful eyes of the security guards by the door.

"Miss King, how are you this evening? Enjoying the music?"

She sipped her martini and examined him. "Do I know you?"

"You will if you keep hanging out with Pete Mintz." He took out his own cigarettes. Lucky Strikes. Not the fancy French brand Miss King was smoking, but Frank wasn't a fancy kind of guy. "You know who your sweetheart is?"

"I know him enough to know that nobody—" Her red-painted lips curled around the word, stretching it. "—calls him a sweetheart."

Her carefully cultivated voice reminded him of an aspiring actress, some small town girl from the middle of the country who caught a bus to LA with big dreams. She paced her words, drawing them out for maximum effect.

And that voice *was* effective, even though Frank knew Nina King was from a little house on the East Side.

She continued, "And who exactly are you, mister?"

"Detective Frank Bogle."

She rolled her eyes. "I don't know who hired you but—"

"The good people of Los Angeles, ma'am," he said. "I'm with the police department."

She paused. "Like I said, I don't know who hired you, but if you have questions about Pete, you ask Pete. Everyone who knows me, knows that."

"I know you might find it hard to believe," he said, "but I'm not on the take. For anyone, including your boyfriend. Everyone who knows *me*, knows that."

She blew out a stream of smoke. "One of the good boys, huh? How sweet."

"That's me," Frank said. "Sweet as candy."

"And just as likely to cost me my teeth," Nina said under her breath. The Hollywood accent slipped. "Why are you here?"

"You're a good girl, Nina. Your family's worried about you."

A flicker in her eyes.

That's right, sweetheart. I've been to that little house on the East Side. Seen the pictures of little Magdalena Reyes there.

"You were cute in your confirmation dress, Nina."

Rage bubbled just under the surface. Rage… and fear.

"You leave my family out of this." She wasn't speaking for the guards anymore. He could barely hear her over the music. " What do you want? You want money? The money is Pete's. I have nothing. You want to make time with me?" The carefully cultivated ennui fell away. "You think he lets me out of his sight? All the guards here report to him, just like they do everywhere. If you think he doesn't know about this meeting, you don't know a thing about Pete Mintz."

"I don't want your money or anything else. I just want you to do the right thing. You know something—like about those murders on the East Side by your ma's house? You tell me."

"You're asking me to snitch?" She lit another cigarette after stabbing out the first. The Hollywood accent was back. "You're delusional, mister."

As she reached forward, Frank's eyes were drawn to the evenly spaced bruises her cap sleeve didn't quite cover.

Damn Pete Mintz to hell. No wonder her ma was crying.

She caught him looking and rearranged her shoulders, draping her wrap over even more evidence of Mintz being an animal. "You done?"

"Maybe." He had to ask. Frank dropped his voice so the moaning saxophone masked his words. "You want out, Nina?"

Nina froze for a second, then she carefully took another drag, blew out the smoke. "Like I said, you're delusional, mister."

She wanted out.

Frank took his card out, flipped it with practiced care under the table, making sure to hit her ankle. She'd pick it up or leave it, but he had to offer. Smooth as silk, he slid out of the booth and buttoned his jacket, nodding politely at Magdalena Reyes before he turned to go.

"Ma'am. Hope you enjoy the music. Have a nice night."

"I'd like to say it was nice meeting you, Detective Bogle." She raised her voice for the guards before she finished one martini and—quick as a blink—another was on the table. "But I'm not that good a liar."

4

What do I know? Not much,
apparently

I COULD TASTE the tobacco on my lips when Frank left my mind. I tried not to gag and took a long drink of the beer I'd set on the table. It was slightly warm, but I didn't care. I drank half of it before I set it down again. Visions like that one left me parched.

I licked my lips and tasted the Lucky Strikes. "So Nina King was a mob moll, huh?"

Frank was sitting in front of me now. He shook his head. "You think that, you didn't see enough."

"Her boyfriend was beating her up?"

He nodded.

"So she'd keep her mouth shut about what she knew?"

"Partly. And partly because Pete Mintz was a piece of shit human being."

Frank rarely used the word shit.

"And she stayed with him," I said.

"It's not that simple."

"So explain it to me, Bogie."

"What I showed you was in 1952, just after a pair of murders on the East Side. The victims were strange. Unexpected, a nice Mexican couple with grown kids. Husband had a steady job. Wife was a seamstress. No criminal connections. Not Mintz's usual type. He was an animal but he didn't kill randomly. He was too smart for that."

"And you were the detective on the case?"

"Yeah."

"Did you solve it?"

He gave me a look and I knew he hadn't.

"Time to read the note?" I asked.

He let out a breath that ghosted across my cheek. Spirits were weird that way. Sometimes their energy was chaotic enough that they could affect the environment. The fact that Frank's energy was so churned up was telling.

I pulled out my phone and zoomed in on the close-up of the letter.

OCTOBER 12, 1952

DEAREST FRANK,

I KNOW this letter might be too little, too late, but it's finally over. I'm done with Pete. He came to me last night and I could see the blood on his hands. I know he killed the Mendez family. It was so awful. When he hit me, blood got on my dress. I don't know if I can ever get the stain out, and I can't live like this anymore.

I'm leaving him. Your love has given me the courage to escape. Meet me at my Aunt Mary's house Friday morning. I should be able to get away then. I'm so afraid, but it's the only way I can live with myself. I can't stay with a murderer.

I love you, Frank. You gave me the courage to do this. I just want to make things right.

ALL MY LOVE,
   Nina King

FRANK WAS STARING at me intently. "You see it, right?"

I was still reeling from the idea of Frank having a lover who was a mobster's girlfriend. As acerbic as he could be, he was as straight an arrow as ever was shot. I mean, if I imagined Frank having a girlfriend, it was the girl-next-door type, not the femme fatale.

I blinked. "What?"

"You see what I spotted immediately, right?"

"Poor Nina got herself killed because she was running away with you?"

He scowled. "Nina King and I were not in love. We never planned on running away with each other."

"But the note—"

"She lied. That's what has me thinking. Yeah, Mintz beat her up. And the thing about the blood on her dress was clearly a hint for me to search her house, which I did when she went missing, but I never found a dress with blood on it. I'd have spotted that. And why'd she sign her name like that if she was pretending we were lovers? Who signs their full name on a love letter?"

I shook off the shock of Frank having an affair with a mobster's girlfriend and tried to think about what else I'd seen. "Uh… so you and she never… Cause I'm not gonna lie. That vision? You two had chemistry."

He looked at me like I'd just slapped my nan. "She was a victim, Linx. Pete Mintz kept her on a leash that was shorter than his… It was short. He was beating her up, threatening her family—"

"How do you know all that?"

"Because she called me from her mother's house two weeks after we met. Once a month, she was allowed to go to her mother's house and she called from there."

"So you did see her?"

"Yeah, but it wasn't…" Frank shook his head. "Nina was smart. Beautiful. But I don't think even she knew who she was anymore." He waved at my phone. "None of that letter makes any sense. It's her handwriting, but it doesn't make sense."

"I don't know." I tried to put together what I knew. "Maybe she really was trying to leave. She was going to send you the letter—"

"How? No address on the envelope."

"Um…" I really wanted to go brush my teeth. The tobacco taste was nauseating. "Her mother? Maybe she was going to give her mom the letter and have her mom get in touch with you. If Mintz checked her mail—"

"Okay." Frank started nodding. "I know he did."

"Then she probably was going to leave the letter with her mom and trust her to give it to you. Maybe she wasn't going to run away with you, but she really wanted to get away from Mintz."

"So why pretend we were lovers?" he asked.

"I don't know, Frank! It's late. I've already committed a felony tonight, hung out in your head, and now I feel like I'm going to gag on my own breath," I protested. "All I want to do is brush my teeth, take a shower, and go to bed."

"Fine." He waved his hand at me. "Whatever. Go to bed if you're tired."

I rolled my eyes. Now he was just being a moody prick. "Fine."

See if I play you any Duke Ellington tomorrow night.

"She didn't even have an Aunt Mary," he muttered.

"Bogie, leave it alone." I stood up and stretched my legs. "She's been dead for sixty years. I don't think taking a break for me to get some sleep is going to change anything."

Despite my annoyance, the look on his face was breaking my heart. I'd never seen him so confused. "I promise we'll work on it tomorrow. Maybe one of Nan's people knows something. We can go take a look around the park if you want. Who knows, maybe Nina's still hanging around."

"Christ, I hope not," he muttered. "She deserved better than that."

He hated being caught here. I knew that. But I didn't know any better than he did why he was stuck with me, and his words stung.

"Goodnight, Frank."

He leaned back and put ghostly elbows on the picnic table, staring up into the night sky and saying nothing.

I walked to the house and turned before I went inside. "We'll figure it out, Bogie. I promise."

5

Same world. Less style

BUT TOMORROW CAME and so did work. Actual paying work, not detective work that put me at risk of arrest, which meant Frank was going to have to be patient. Jackson had called me to the cafe with the other artists, and it was a good thing he did, because artistic temperaments were as bad as moody ghosts.

Farah was pacing at the back of the bookstore, his dark, beautiful eyes glaring. I was trying to take his tantrum seriously, but he was just so pretty.

"Do I have to go? Why do I have to go? People will just spend all night asking me if the red represents blood when I mean…" He gestured at his section of the wall. "I mean, really? You have to ask?"

Jackson was on the other side of the store drumming his fingers on the nearly finished counter, most of the crew was gone, and my other friends, Cristiane, Jonny, and Randy, were hanging around in the lounge area. I had silently checked all of them for wet paint and I couldn't find any, so I wasn't too worried about the new—and very expensive looking—easy chairs.

"Dude, chill," I said. "You're getting yourself all worked up for no reason. Jackson invited us to be polite. The cafe opening is like… it's kind of like a gallery opening for overly caffeinated people. I mean, our wall kicks ass and we do too. And he kind of went out on a limb doing something different here instead of the happy scene of busy urban life, you know? He invited us out of respect."

Farah still looked confused. "Are you going?"

"Of course I am. And I'm bringing business cards. Which is something you should do, too."

He looked so appalled. Poor anti-social Farah. People would flock to him to ask about the blood thing. Of course, he'd also get hit on. He was beautiful and his eyelashes alone made me want to stab him.

In the most loving way possible.

He said, "My stuff is never going to be popular like yours and Jonny's, okay? No one wants my business card, Linx. I appreciate you tagging me for this project, but we both know I'm still going to be working at my dad's office next week."

I actually thought Farah's dad was kind of awesome. If he was my dad, I'd probably be willing to work in the family business, too, even if it was an accounting firm.

That was a lie. I suck at math. But I did think Farah's dad was awesome.

"Your stuff is amazing, okay? And maybe you're not as commercial as I am, or Jonny is, but your painting is the kind that people talk about for days after they see it."

"Because it disturbs them."

"Because it's *amazing*." It was amazing. And disturbing. But good art should be disturbing at times. It should make you think. "Listen, you don't have to go. I'd like for you to be there—I think it'd be great for your career—but you don't have to be."

The relief was visible. "Is Jackson going to be offended? I mean, he's a capitalist, but not the worst kind. I didn't mind working on his wall."

I thought it was ironic that Farah helped people sort out their taxes and hated capitalism so much, but what did I know? Maybe depriving the government of tax revenue was anarchic in its own way.

"I'm sure he'll be cool with it. I'll handle Jackson."

Farah's cheeky humor finally reemerged. "I bet you will."

"Get your mind out of the gutter."

"Have you seen my paintings? My mind is always in the gutter, baby."

"Whatever, my twisted Persian Picasso."

Farah leaned over whispered in my ear. "Think if I stay like this and keep talking he'll get jealous?"

Maybe? I could tell Jackson was watching us. "Stop."

"Why?" His breath was hot on my neck. "You smell good, Linx. Were you smoking last night? You bad girl. You know that turns me on."

I slapped his hip to get him away, and also because yeah, I was turned on. Farah was temperamental as shit, but he was hot. He was also smart, and his sly humor cracked me up when it made an appearance. We'd made out more than once but had never gone farther. What we had was friendly, and I didn't want to risk our working relationship, even if Farah was dazzling and addictive when he was in a good mood.

I asked, "Are you coming or not?"

"Not yet. But with a little encouragement…"

"Give it a rest. Real answer, please?"

He sighed. "I'll… make an appearance."

"Lucky us." I tried not to roll my eyes. "I'll let Jackson know. Want to…" I was going to say 'grab lunch with the others,' but I felt Frank's chill on the back of my neck.

"Linx, you okay?"

"Yeah." I stretched my neck from side to side. "Just slept funny last night. No comments." I held up a hand. "I need to go. I promised my nan I'd help her with something."

"Okay, I'll see you on Friday." He brushed a kiss over my cheek. Just to be Farah. And also probably because Cristiane was looking at us and she'd had the hots for him since art school.

Not wanting to awkwardly flirt with Jackson in front of my friends, I made my excuses, promised to see everyone Friday night, and then headed out to my van. Frank was waiting for me in the passenger's seat.

"You know, I kinda like that Farah kid."

"That Farah kid is nearly thirty, and *what*?" I blinked when I digested his words. "Farah? You don't like Jackson —you hated Gus—"

"Gus stole your car."

"He returned it!"

"After he broke the transmission."

Okay, Frank was right. Gus had been an asshole.

"You don't like the boy scout, but you think Farah's a good bet?"

Frank lifted an eyebrow. "He'd keep you on your toes."

I started my car. "I don't know what Nan was thinking; you are no judge of character at all."

~O~

IT WAS ONLY ONCE I got on the highway I asked him where we were going.

"Park or library?"

He thought for a moment. "Library. I don't think we'll find anything at the park. She wasn't killed there."

"How do you know?"

"Because that's where Mintz buried his bodies, not where he killed 'em."

I shook my head. "Sometimes it's hard to imagine your world."

"Same world you live in, kid." He nodded at a billboard advertising 'LIVE GIRLS.' "Yours just has a lot less style."

I couldn't argue with him.

We pulled into the library and I parked in my regular spot. Frank and I spent a lot of time at the library. He was way more patient than I was, but that could have been the 'being dead' thing. I'd asked him once what he did when he wasn't with me. I'll never forget his response.

"I wait."

I hope I'm never a ghost. Whatever light comes toward me when I die, I'm running toward it, and with all the masses I'd attended and all the rosaries I'd been forced to say over the years, Saint Peter had better let me in.

Frank and I headed toward the computers because that's where all the old newspapers are kept.

What? You mean I didn't have to look through dusty old rooms? Nope. The LA County Library system was one of the best in the world.

Here's the thing.

I could access *all* this information from my house with a library card number. In fact, it'd be a lot easier there. Two things kept me coming back to the library computers for research. One, when I worked in the library, Frank didn't argue with me, because it's the library and even dead, he was a rule-follower. And two, Frank *loved* the library. I don't know if he was a bookworm in life or if he just likes the odd mix of people you run into there, but every time we walked in, he emanated a really happy energy.

I saw in an isolated corner and pulled out my notebook. I couldn't talk on my phone to hide my conversations with him at the library, so I wrote notes or just mumbled questions. You could get away with talking to yourself (some) at the public library. Today, I opted for notes.

What are we looking for?

"Search for August 1952. Los Angeles Times. Murder on East Side."

I started searching, clicking and opening and closing and scrolling page after page.

"Stop," Frank said, pointing toward the screen. "That one."

I clicked on the PDF.

"It wasn't on the front page," he said. "Yankees beat by the Tigers in a no-hitter that day."

"How do you remember this stuff?" I whispered.

"What else do I have to do." His hand lifted. "There. Toward the bottom."

My mouth dropped. "A whole family murdered in their home didn't go on the front page?" One thing I'd learned from hanging out with Frank was that once upon a time, most murders were front page news, not only the ones involving celebrities.

"It was buried. Mintz had connections at the paper." He leaned forward. "And the department."

"So what—"

"Read the article, kid. Then ask your questions."

There wasn't much to read, but what was there was horrifying. This was another strange crime, like the one he'd mentioned before. A husband, wife, and their two daughters had been stabbed to death in their home in East LA. The husband worked in a factory. The wife worked for a dry-cleaner. Both their little girls attended the local elementary school and were reported to be excellent students.

A dry-cleaning shop.

"*...a nice Mexican couple with grown kids. Husband had a steady job. Wife was a seamstress.*"

I tapped the notebook to get his attention. *First female victim was a seamstress,* I wrote. *Next one worked in a dry-cleaners.*

Could they have known each other? Did dry-cleaners hire seamstresses back then?

"Yeah, they did." He rubbed his chin out of habit. "I haven't looked at the details on that case in a long time. Hadn't thought of that."

Could Mintz had wanted them dead for some reason? Why would he drop off his cleaning in East LA? He didn't live there, did he?

"Nah, he lived in Pasadena."

I whispered, "And it always seemed like such a nice neighborhood."

Frank smirked. "It was. Mintz was probably the best neighbor you ever had as long as you didn't cross him."

So again, why would he have his dry-cleaning in East LA.?

"Because of Nina?"

"Maybe she dropped something off," I whispered, "when she was at her mom's? Those two women found something or saw something."

Someone shot me a dirty look.

I wrote, *Let's go back to my house.*

"We need to talk," Frank said. "And kid, I think you need a smoke."

Dammit.

6

Secrets kill

FRANK WAS WAITING in the back of Esmerelda Reyes's closet. The front of the woman's house was watched every time her daughter came to visit, so Frank had snuck in the night before to wait. It was just a good thing Mrs. Reyes and Frank were on the same page about Nina. Drawn curtains would have been noticed around the rest of the house, but not in the older woman's bedroom. Hiding in there gave Frank and Nina a window to talk in private.

"Frank?"

He'd become familiar with her whisper. What he hadn't gotten used to was the quick tightening of need it provoked. Ignoring it, he cracked the door open. "I'm here."

She let out a breath she'd been holding and sat on the edge of the bed. He watched her, knowing that these stolen moment with him were some of the few truly private moments she owned. He was intruding, but he couldn't find it in himself to care.

"Did you hear?"

"About the Mendez family?"

Frank nodded.

"Yeah." She looked shaky. Thin. The stress was getting to her. Her face had lost its glow and the generous curves had shrunk to nothing. If she kept going like this, she wouldn't have to worry about getting away from Mintz; he'd dump her and move on to a new piece.

Maybe that was her plan.

"Can you give me anything, Nina? Anything to take to the District Attorney? We don't have any proof, but we know it's him."

"Everybody knows it's him," she said. "That's the point, isn't it?"

"And no one's talking."

"Yeah, well, that's the thing." There were bruises beneath her eyes. "None of us really want to wind up dead, do we?"

She knew something. He was sure of it. She had something they could use to nail the bastard. "Nina, I can protect you."

"I got a family, Frank. You gonna protect them, too? I got a kid brother who goes to school and works for a stone mason on weekends. You can't watch him every day. My papa may be gone, but my mama's still hanging on. What are you going to do for them, huh?"

"These are innocent people, Nina. People in your own neighborhood. Families. Children. This is not Mintz playing the game. These are civilians, and you know this isn't right."

She let out a breath and her shoulders slumped. "It

doesn't matter. I don't have any proof, Frank. And I don't have time to… I can't give you my testimony because I didn't see anything. I hear things, but he doesn't trust me. I don't see anything anymore. I'm just there to… you know."

If you were mine, I'd wake up singing.

The thought jumped into his mind, and his thumb slid over Nina's cheek, brushed the shadows under her eyes. "I'll figure it out. I'll figure out a way to put him away."

I'll make you safe.

"It doesn't matter," she murmured. "Doesn't matter anymore."

"Sleep, doll. I'll keep an eye out for your ma."

She didn't argue. Nina slid her shoes off and crawled into her mother's bed, curling up like a child as Frank laid a blanket over her.

"Sweet dreams, Nina."

7

A visit to Aunt Mary's house

I CAME out of the vision coughing. The smoke was in my mouth. My lungs. My hair. I held up a hand before Frank started speaking and walked inside. I needed a minute to breathe. I needed a minute to think. I walked up to my room and the door closed in my mind while I took a shower. Frank respected my privacy and didn't make an appearance.

There were a few things about Frank's visions that he didn't know. One, he didn't know how far I was in his head when I had them. For instance, I'm pretty sure he didn't intend to show me how much he was feeling for Nina King. No matter how much he might play the honorable knight—and he *was* honorable—he also had feelings for the woman. Two, I don't think he realized that I remembered everything. And I mean everything. Whatever he showed me ended up glued in my head in detail I normally didn't recall in my own life, much less someone else's.

There was something about her appearance that was bugging me. I got out of the shower, got dressed and started drying my hair, still mulling it over. I couldn't put my finger on it. I walked back down to the backyard after putting on a pair of shorts and a ratty concert tee I'd had since high school. Frank was waiting for me, but whatever I was seeing hadn't coalesced yet.

"She knew something," I said.

"She said she didn't, but I could tell she was hiding something."

"Would it have even worked? Having her testify against him? Would she have been a credible witness?"

Did it matter anymore? I'd looked up Mintz on my own. The crime boss had been killed only a year after Frank must have died in 1953. And because fate had a sense of humor, Mintz had died in an automobile collision.

Yep. The murderous crime boss died in a car crash.

In my head, I was hoping someone cut his brakes in revenge or something.

Nina King was still dead. Her murderer was still dead. And we were trying to solve the mystery… why?

Because of that damn note.

I sat down on the picnic bench and drummed my fingers on the table. There were too many threads to pull. Too many questions and only Frank to answer them. "Bogie, what was the thing you were saying about Nina's aunt?"

"What?" He'd been staring at my drumming fingers. "Oh, Nina didn't have an Aunt Mary. She had an Aunt *Maria*, but that was her mother's sister and she was dead.

The woman died of cancer years before Nina ever met Mintz. They were close, but it had been years since Maria had died."

"Huh." I leaned my elbows on the table. "'Meet me at my Aunt Mary's house Friday morning.'"

"It makes no sense."

"But Aunt Mary has to be Maria, right?"

"Yeah, but the note—"

"I know," I said. "It doesn't make any sense."

The note might not have made sense, but there were a few things we did know. Nina was leaving Mintz. Mintz got word of it and killed her. According to Raul, she'd had a bullet in her head. Mintz had buried the body in Griffith Park. Frank had gone looking for her when she disappeared. And when he'd gone looking…

"Hey, Frank." I felt like it was time to ask. "How did you die?"

"Mintz killed me." His voice didn't sound rough, because… well, he didn't really have a throat, did he? But his energy felt rough. Brittle.

"I was looking for Nina," he said. "I was hoping that she'd just taken off, you know? First time I remember praying in… I don't know how long. I was praying she'd gotten away from that bastard."

"Her family didn't know?"

"They knew." He stared at the table, his shoulders slumped. His fedora, usually tipped back at a cocky angle, hung over his eyes. "In the back of my mind, I knew. Her mother started leaving flowers on her sister's grave. She hadn't done that in years. But I knew… it was for both of them. If Nina had taken off, she'd have told her ma and her brother. But she didn't, and Mintz never came by to harass them."

"Because he knew she was dead."

He nodded. "I knew he'd killed her, but I couldn't prove it."

Meet me at my Aunt Mary's house.

"Frank, do you remember what cemetery Nina's aunt was buried in?"

———

THE GATES of Calvary Cemetery in East LA were open when we swung off Whittier Boulevard and into the spacious, park-like resting place for thousands of Los Angeles Catholics. East LA had always been a multi-ethnic neighborhood, and the graves reflected it.

"Does it look much different?" I asked Frank, who was staring out the car window.

"Not really." He sat low in the seat, staring at the sunlit graveyard.

He was more transparent than usual.

I tried to lighten the mood. "I can't believe you remember where her grave is."

"The only thing I do is remember." He angled his neck to look at something that I'd just passed. "Jeez, I recognized that name. Arrested a guy with that name when he was a punk kid."

"Think it's the same one?"

"Could be."

He wasn't his usual talkative self. Frank loved regaling me with collar stories from back in the day. He had a dry sense of humor and an appreciation for the absurd. Today, he clearly wasn't feeling it.

By the time we parked the car, the sun was starting to set behind the chapel I could see in the distance. I stepped over graves that weren't so carefully tended and some that were immaculate.

Maria Cordoba's grave had the grass trimmed around it, but there were no flowers to be found. I pulled out the small metal detector I'd brought in the car.

"Jeez, kid, are you seriously going to…" Frank tugged off his hat, then put it back on again, pacing a little. "That's not respectful, you know?"

"Meet me at Aunt Mary's house," I said. "It was obviously a clue."

"Yeah, for me to meet her here. But she got killed before it happened." His mouth twisted. "I don't even know why you wanted to come here."

Sometimes, Bogie…

I dropped the metal detector on the ground. "We're following this whole thing because of the note, right? We're trying to figure out what Nina meant by that note."

"I know what she meant," Frank said bitterly. "She wanted to leave him, and I didn't get the message."

If I could have punched him, I would have. "So what's the point, Frank? We know who killed Nina. We know who killed you. Mintz is dead. So why are we bothering? We're not trying to find answers for anyone living, are we?"

He stood there silently, his hands in his pockets.

I looked around, but we were completely alone. Nobody could see me ranting like a crazy person. "I'm doing this for you, okay? To help you find peace or resolution or… whatever, but I'm doing all this for you. Do you want me to drop it?"

He still said nothing.

"Seriously?"

Nada. Zip. Zilch. He wasn't even looking at me anymore. He was staring at the Calvary Cemetery chapel, watching the sun go down.

"You're such a jerk, Bogie."

I shook my head, picked up my metal detector, and started walking back to the car. This was ridiculous. I was trying to solve a mystery that didn't need to be solved. Everyone it mattered to was dead, including the guy who bugged me about it to begin with. Maybe he couldn't stand to let the past lie, but I could.

I was done with his baggage. I had a life. I had a job.

I was done.

8

Life and other stunning revelations

BY FRIDAY, I was ready for the week to end. I dressed up for the opening of the cafe, but my heart wasn't in it. I couldn't get excited about the event. Sure, I wanted to flirt with Jackson. And okay, maybe Farah. But it wasn't as much fun without my Bogie, and Frank hadn't made an appearance since I left him at the cemetery.

I was pissed, but I was still feeling mopey about going to the party without Frank. After all, when I was with my bogie, I was never alone. Even if my company was dead.

Maybe I needed to work on that. I made a mental note to look up "co-dependency" online.

The black sheath dress was ripped across the middle, which would normally leave my belly showing, but I had personal issues with showing skin. My nan had sewed a panel across it made from sari fabric she'd bought in India when she went a few years before. The fabric made the dress bohemian. The rips made it punk. Exactly how I liked it. I grabbed my purse and headed downstairs, waving to my mom and nan as I left.

"Is Frank going with you?" Mom called.

"Nope!" And I didn't care. Which was a total lie. I even found myself taking a deep breath by someone who was smoking yesterday.

Definitely look up co-dependency.

It was Friday night, but traffic wasn't completely awful, so I made it to the cafe in under an hour. Parking took almost as long, but the wait was worth it. I stepped in and immediately felt like a rock star.

Jackson had put a picture of the five of us—Farah, Jonny, Cristiane, Randy, and me—on a placard by our wall. It was a promotional shot we'd done at our last collective meeting and my hair was a vivid purple. People all over the cafe were staring at the wall and pointing out different elements of the project. Farah's section had the biggest crowd—he was already holding reluctant court in the corner—but my portrait gallery had a pretty decent audience, too. Cristiane waved and gave me a big smile and a thumbs up I returned.

I grabbed a glass of red wine and allowed myself to flow with the audience. I waved at acquaintances and shook lots of hands, answered questions about my painting and my background in LA. I was a native, therefore I was a curiosity to the imports. And there were so many imports. I ended up mingling in a group of Jackson's friends from the east coast. Ten minutes into the conversation, I'd made myself at home as the random colorful local.

Apparently, Jackson had lived in Brooklyn before he'd

moved to LA. But that was 'so over' and he was loving the opportunities on the west coast. His mother in Omaha must have thought the people were friendlier, too. Had I met her yet? Because apparently she was great.

If I thought it was a little odd how familiar Jackson's friends had instantly become, it felt even more odd when he came up beside me and draped an arm over my shoulder.

I babbled incoherently. In my head.

"You met Linx, I see." He was all smiles and good humor. "You guys all saw the wall, right?"

"So amazing."

"Darkness and light."

"Dynamic."

"Such a great idea to capture the urban aesthetic with street art instead of the usual…" *Blah blah blah.*

I'd heard art-speak before, and I'm not gonna lie, who doesn't love compliments? But it was Jackson's glowing face I couldn't stop returning to. He was just so nice. And I liked nice! He was smart. Accomplished. Ambitious without being an asshole. Beyond the crush-on-the-cute-boy thing, I realized that I could really, really like this guy.

"Linx!"

I turned toward the familiar voice. "Raul?"

I made my excuses with Jackson and his friends, then walked over to the bar. Raul was standing there with a date.

"Hey, gorgeous," he said. "This is Langdon. Lang, this is Linx."

Langdon looked about as interested in meeting me as he was in the wine he wasn't drinking.

I shook hands with him anyway. "Hi!"

Langdon looked over the party. Clearly, I wasn't the most interesting thing there.

Raul smirked at him and walked away with me. "He's pretty."

"Then you match. What are you doing here?" I asked.

"You talked about this place so much, I called and asked if I could come." He looked around and sipped his glass of red. "Amazing, baby. Those eyes are insane and crazy and I love them. Farah really needs to stop with the blood, though." Raul made a face. "So hot, yet so emo."

"Wait." I frowned. "I thought this was invite-only."

He sipped his wine. "It is."

"So how did you get in?"

"I called them and asked if I could come."

"You just… called up and asked if you could come to the private opening of a cafe to which you have no real connection?"

"Yes. I called the number listed on the website and a girl answered." He plucked a passing chocolate truffle. "I told her I was a friend of yours, I drink a lot of coffee, and I have fifty thousand followers on Instagram. Also that I was hot and was bringing a hot date. Could they put me on the guest list please?"

It could never be said that Raul lacked confidence. I'd never even thought about doing that before, just calling and inviting myself to parties. I wondered if it would work in galleries.

"Wait." I blinked. "You have fifty *thousand* followers on Instagram?"

"Yep."

I might need to get more Instagram fans. I think I had closer to five thousand, and half of those were spam accounts. Of course, I also didn't look like Adonis or have a washboard stomach. Raul had me beat there.

"So whatever happened with glamor girl?" he asked. "Did you and your mysterious sources find anything we didn't know already?"

Yes, but not anything I can share with people who don't see dead people.

"Doubt it," I said. "I thought there was a story but—"

"Oh! I did want to tell you that if you wanted to see her medical records, the paper-chasers found them. I could get a copy for you. I didn't even know hospitals kept records that far back, but I guess they have to."

I blinked. "Medical records?"

"Yeah, because of the cancer."

Whoa. Record scratch. *What?*

"What cancer?" I asked.

He frowned. "I thought you knew. I mean, the pathologist thought it probably started out as ovarian cancer, but it had gone into her bones, so by the time she died and you could see— Oh!" He snapped his fingers. "That's right, you didn't want to see the bones. I forgot about that."

"Nina King had cancer?" *Shit shit shit.*

"Bone cancer. Sad, right? I saw a picture of her they found in the police file. She was a knockout. I guess it sounds like the guy who killed her was a real asshole, but you probably knew that."

This changed… What? What did it change?

One of those threads was waving in the wind, practically begging for me to tug it, but there was something I wasn't seeing.

Raul continued, "The pathologist said it looks like she'd have been dead within six months if she hadn't been murdered.

Oh. OH.

I *had* seen it.

And so had Frank.

She'd been so thin. It wasn't from stress like Frank thought. It hadn't been the stress. Nina had been sick, and she knew it.

I don't have time…

It doesn't matter anymore.

'Meet me at Aunt Mary's house.'

I handed Raul my wine. "I gotta go."

9

The Note

I'M NOT GOING to lie about climbing over fences. Considering the people I hung out with in high school... I'd climbed over a lot. Chain link was obviously the easiest, but the fence at Calvary Cemetery shouldn't have been that big a deal. And it wouldn't have been if I wasn't wearing a dress.

Let's just say that if you were hanging out on South Eastern Avenue on Friday night, you got a show. Hope you enjoyed my Spanx. You're welcome.

I landed on the grass and grabbed the duffel bag I'd thrown over, then I made my way across the black graveyard.

Spooky? Not really. Graveyards at night were usually pretty peaceful, but they were hard to navigate. I found the main path and made my way north to the baby angel playing a harp by a bench. Then I turned right and followed the path I'd first walked with Bogie days before.

Maria Cordoba's grave didn't look any different than it

had the other day, but this time, I'd come prepared. I still had my metal detector, but I also stuffed a few more things in my backpack. Lock picks (thanks, granddad), a penlight, and various blades I could use to pry things up. I was thinking Nina had buried a lockbox of some kind, but there was no way of being sure until I looked.

Whatever I was looking for was something Frank was meant to find. As soon as I learned about the cancer, something in me knew that Nina King had never intended to meet Frank Bogle at her aunt's grave. Nina had left the note because she wanted Frank there for another reason. She left a message to confuse him because she knew Frank well enough to know that he was a bulldog about finding the truth. Leaving a confusing note was like throwing red meat to a tiger.

I looked around, but the Calvary Cemetery was silent to me. If my nan had been there, she'd probably have a field day. Ghosts love to hang out where people spent a lot of energy on their memory, and very little drew as much emotional energy as their grave. But I didn't feel anything around Maria Cordoba's grave, not when I searched with my flashlight. Not when I got down on my knees with the metal detector.

I kept waiting for Frank to pop in—I'd thrown the door wide open on my end—but he hadn't. A tiny frightened part of me wondered if he'd moved on. He couldn't. Not until he knew the truth.

Nina hadn't been a victim. Not at the end.

The metal detector wasn't giving me any love, not even near the base of the gravestone. I didn't want to dig up the whole area, so I grabbed the ice pick I brought from my Nan's kitchen and methodically pushed it into the soil all around the stone.

Still nothing.

If there was something buried, I was missing it.

Words from Frank's last memory of Nina drifted through my mind: *'I got a brother who works for a stone mason…'*

Ah ha.

I grabbed the penlight and shone it on the base of the Maria's grave. Inch by inch I crawled along the base of the marker, wiping away grass clippings and dirt to reveal the marble.

It was in the center of the back that I found the seam. I grabbed my pocketknife and scraped at the edges, revealing a thin rectangle, almost the same dimensions as a letterbox. I managed to work the tip of the blade into the seam and wiggled it to loosen the marble.

Whoever Nina's brother was, I hope he went on to a long and successful career, because that was some seriously detailed work.

It must have been an hour later that I managed to work the marble cover from the gravestone. It was only half an inch thick and concealed a small crevice where a rolled up piece of paper was wrapped in yellowed cellophane. The cellophane cracked as I rolled it open, but the stationery was the same as the letter found with Nina's body and showed very few signs of age.

I felt Frank's cool presence settle beside me on the grass.

"She was sick," I said. "Cancer. Raul told me tonight. She had six months at the most."

His energy spiked, but I didn't see him move and he didn't speak.

I carefully unrolled the note and held the penlight up so I could read it aloud.

"DEAR FRANK,

IF YOU FOUND THIS, then I'm dead and you got the note. I hope it doesn't get you in too much trouble, but it seemed a more likely story if I was running away with a lover when Pete found me. I knew you and my mother would be able to back up the story in court if you needed to.

Did you figure it out, Frankie? I'm trying my best, but I've never framed a man for murder before. I just hope it works and someone finally throws Pete Mintz in a hole. God knows I haven't done anything worth much in this life. Maybe I can do something with my death.

I'm done, Frank. I've known for months, but I couldn't tell you. That night at the club, I wanted to, but I couldn't.

Thank you. For everything. If you can watch out for my mama and Eddie, I'd appreciate it. I think Eddie knows something is up, but he doesn't look at me the same way as he used to. Doesn't see me.

No one does, not even you.

If we'd met in a different life, we could have talked about music instead of murder. We could have danced some more.

Maybe if I do things right, I'll meet you in the next one, handsome.

ALL MY LOVE,
  Nina"

I WIPED AWAY the tears and sniffed loudly. I felt a cold brush along my back. Frank's version of a hug.

"She killed herself." I sniffed. "She wasn't a victim, Frank. She tried to put Mintz away so he couldn't hurt anyone else."

"When did you know?"

"When Raul told me about the cancer. She was so thin in your last memory. As soon as he told me, I put it together."

He was silent for a long time.

"I didn't see it," he said softly.

"You were trying to catch the bad guy." I shrugged. "You had a job to do."

"But she was my friend."

The way he said it, I wondered if he'd ever admitted it aloud. "Just a friend?"

He stared at the note on my lap. "You got my cigarettes?"

I pulled a box out of my backpack. "I've been carrying them around for a couple days."

"Light up, kid."

10

I like the sunrise

FRANK WAITED for her steps to near, then he opened the door to the dark hallway and pulled Nina into the broom closet near the ladies' room. She tried to scream, but he put his hand over her mouth and turned her quickly. Her terror died when she saw him.

"Frank," she hissed. "What are you doing? Pete's got guys all over this club. You trying to get me killed?"

"You didn't go to your ma's."

There was something in her eyes, but he couldn't figure it out. He was too wracked with worry. Until she'd walked into the jazz club on Mintz's arm that night, he'd thought the worst. Nina never missed a visit with her mother. Even when her brother had stopped coming, she never missed a visit. Bruises. Bleeding lips. Black eyes. Frank sometimes thought Mintz messed up her face just to humiliate Nina in front of her family.

But that night, there were no bruises—not even a trace of them as he examined her—but she still hadn't come.

She lifted her chin. "I had… a thing. Something I needed to do."

"Something more important than visiting your ma?"

His hand was on her wrist, and he felt the pulse pick up.

"Nina, what's going on?"

She opened her mouth, but nothing came out. Tears flooded her eyes.

"Nina?" An entirely unprofessional panic nearly stole his breath. "Tell me what's wrong."

She shook her head. "I can't. I can't."

Frank took her in his arms. He'd have given anything at that moment—his body, his badge, *anything*—to save her.

He just had to fix this. Put the bastard away. If he put Mintz away, she could have a life again. She could put herself back together. They could…

It wasn't about that. It couldn't be about that. He was doing the right thing. That was all.

The right thing.

"Dance with me, Frankie?"

He opened his eyes. Nina looked up with those dark eyes that killed him. "What?"

"Just dance with me." She tried to smile. "Nobody ever dances with me, and they're playing my favorite song."

Frank heard the bass saxophone moaning from the stage before the singer started in on "I Like the Sunrise." Without another word, he took Nina's hand in his and drew her close, wrapping an arm around her waist as she laid her head on his shoulder.

They swayed in the darkness, the music lifting them out of the dirty club and the crooked city that trapped them. He pressed a kiss to the top of her head, felt her hand clench around his.

"In another life," she whispered. "I bet we'd be all right, handsome."

Frank said nothing. The lump in his throat hurt too damn much.

11

Cigarettes stink and Bogie lies

I LIT another cigarette as we looked over the hills, the Hollywood sign and the sunrise at our back. I blew the smoke in Frank's direction as he watched the morning light start to illuminate the city.

"You can see everything from up here," I said.

Frank leaned against a rock and appeared to take a deep breath. "Everything that matters, kid."

The tobacco coated my tongue, but I figure if anyone had earned a few puffs of nasty, cancer-inducing smoke in their direction, it was Frank. The city stretched before us, downtown to the beach. The lights were flickering off and a new day was coming.

"So you're buried up here, huh?"

He nodded toward a rise just above Mount Lee Drive that was well away from any of the gullies that regularly swept rainwater down the hills and into Griffith Park.

"Not bad, Detective Bogle. If your bones need to rest

somewhere, the hill under the Hollywood sign is pretty cool."

"Yeah, I'm not complaining."

"We could get you down from here," I said. "You want me to send an anonymous tip?"

"Why bother?" He shrugged. "I got a better view than any of the guys who made it to retirement."

"Good point." I glanced at him from the corner of my eye. "No family?"

He shook his head. "Only child."

"We let it lie, then."

"Let it lie." He took another breath of the smoke I blew his direction. "It's good to know. Thanks."

"About Nina?"

He nodded.

"She wasn't a victim."

The corner of his mouth turned up. "No, she wasn't. Mintz must have found her. Buried her in the park to cover his ass. He wouldn't want it getting out his girl killed herself."

"I know what she was trying to do, but I don't get how." I'd been thinking about it since we found Nina's last note to Frank. "Even if she committed suicide and tried to frame Mintz for it, she'd have a hard time leaving her body somewhere his people weren't going to find it."

"True," Frank said. "But I think she must have done it at home. The guards Mintz had on her covered the house, but they didn't go inside. Her neighbors knew her. Liked her. I think most of them knew what was going on."

"So if one of them heard the shot and called the police, they would have pointed at Mintz. And Mintz's guards would be expected to lie about him not being there."

"They'd have been unreliable witnesses," Frank said. "Every one of them had arrest records."

"So according to her plan, she'd take her own life. One of her neighbors would call the police. They'd probably call *you*, in fact. The note would be found in her purse."

"The dress she mentioned might have been the one she was wearing."

"Which would have had someone else's blood on it." I glanced at Bogie. "She knew she could count on you to find it."

"It was a good plan," he said quietly. "Good plan, doll."

He wasn't talking to me anymore.

"What went wrong?" I asked.

"Nobody heard her." He looked at me. Shrugged. "Nobody heard her."

"Yeah."

What else was there to say?

Nina King was a victim. And then she wasn't. I hated the way she'd died, but I had to respect her for it. Had to respect the woman who wanted to make something of her death, even if she'd felt like a failure in life. I watched the sun touch the top of the skyscrapers downtown and realized I agreed with Frank.

I hoped Nina had found peace. And I really hoped she wasn't a ghost.

"So why'd you lie to me, Bogie?"

He frowned. "I never lied to you."

"You told me you and Nina weren't in love."

His face was carefully blank. "I wasn't lying."

I didn't say anything, but I did light another cigarette and blow the smoke toward him.

"She didn't love me, Linx. Like I said, Nina didn't even know who she was anymore."

"If you say so."

A wry chuckle came from Frank's throat. "Kid, what you don't know about love… is a lot."

"Whatever you say, Bogie."

I carefully stubbed out the last of the cigarette and put the butt in the trash bag I'd brought. Cigarettes were gross and I wasn't going to leave any behind in the park, even if other people did. Besides, they were a fire hazard. I stood up, dusted off the back of my ruined dress, and stood just as the sun was breaking over the horizon.

"We solved your mystery, Detective. I found your grave—"

"I showed you my grave." Frank stood at my side, watching the sun rise. "There wasn't much detecting in that one."

"We solved the mystery of who killed you."

He stuck his hands in his pockets. "Which I already knew."

"And we solved the case you were working on when you were killed."

Frank nodded. "We did do that."

"The million-dollar question is: Are you still stuck to me?"

He started to fade in the morning light, tipping his

fedora as he dissolved. "I guess we'll find out. See ya, Linx."

"Bye, Bogie."

———

I SLEPT most of that day. Woke in the afternoon, texted Jackson to apologize for ditching early the night before, then I went back to bed. I kept the door open.

I didn't sense Frank.

I woke up the following morning to the smell of cigarette smoke in my bedroom. I didn't know if that was from the reeking dress in the hamper or—

"Morning, Cupcake."

I groaned and rolled over to face the corner where Frank usually hung out. Sure enough, there he was, sitting in the lime green chair I'd painted the summer before. I blinked when I realized he was wearing a new suit. Navy blue instead of grey pin-stripe.

Dammit, I was actually glad to see him.

"You know what?" I rubbed my eyes. "I'm the one who found Nina's second note. I think you could at least call me partner."

"You want me to call you Partner Cupcake?"

"I take it someone is feeling sassy this morning."

"And someone is still in bed."

"Shut up, Frank."

"Can I point out that if you'd looked at the bones that very first night at the morgue when I told you to we would have figured this out days ago?"

Shit.

"No." I rolled over and gave him my back. "You cannot point that out."

He flicked a piece of ghostly lint off his lapel. "Pretty sure I just did."

"Hey, Frank."

"What?"

I stuck my nose up and sniffed the air. "Smell that?"

"You trying to be cute?"

"Mmmmm. Coffee." I sat up and swung my legs out of bed. "Smells like Nan's already got coffee made. Want a cup? Oh wait—" I stood and walked toward the door. "—you can't have a cup of coffee because you're dead."

"I should have walked toward the light." He followed me out of the bedroom and down the stairs. "I felt the pull. Heard the angels singing. Should have walked toward the light."

"You know you'd miss me, Bogie."

I turned at the base of the stairs and looked up. Frank stood a few steps above me, fighting a smile.

"Whatever you say, kid."

Preview: A Bogie in the Boat

---

*Read ahead for the next chapter in the
Linx and Bogie Mysteries!*

It was Saturday morning at my grandmother's house, and Bogie and I were reading the paper. Or rather, I was trying to read the paper and Bogie was—

"Page," he barked.

I rolled my eyes, reached over, and turned the page of the Sports section. It was the only part of the paper Frank ever wanted to read, but since he was a ghost, he couldn't exactly turn the pages himself. I picked up my mobile phone and added an event to my calendar for the next weekend. The editor had called the exhibit at LACMA "pretentious and unmoving." Maybe it made me "perverse and masochistic," but reviews like that made me want to see it more.

"Page."

"I am not your secretary," I muttered. Then I turned

the page anyway. It was easier than listening to him complain.

"If you were my secretary, I'd fire you for having pink hair." He was wearing a pin-striped navy suit that morning. I'm sure any secretary Detective Frank Bogle'd had in his abbreviated life would have been dressed as snazzily as Frank. Pencil skirt, stylish blouse, and horn-rimmed glasses maybe. A no-nonsense gal for a no-nonsense detective. The thought made me smile.

"What are you smiling about?"

"Did you even have a secretary?"

"The department did. Dora." His slightly transparent form shivered. "She was terrifying but efficient."

"Yeah." I turned the page and skimmed my finger down the upcoming events. "I'd suck at being a secretary." My finger stopped at a mention of the Egyptian Theatre in Hollywood. "Hey! *The Big Heat* is playing next Sunday at the Egyptian."

That pulled his attention away from the football scores. "Really?"

"Yeah, you want to— Ah, shit. Next Sunday is Farah's opening in Santa Monica. We can't go."

Frank gave me a dirty look and looked back at his paper. "Page."

He was pissed off at me, but I couldn't do anything about that. I'd promised Farah when I saw him last week. Unfortunately, Frank wasn't the kind of ghost who could go where he wanted. He was stuck with me.

In truth, most ghosts didn't have that kind of freedom. My grandmother saw spirits who were attached to geography, places that held special meaning for them in life. My mother connected with ghosts who hung around loved ones. Well, usually it was loved ones. Sometimes ghosts hung around hated ones. Those ghosts were a lot less fun.

And I had Frank. Just Frank. He was my bogie, had been since I was thirteen. According to my nan, not one of the Maxwell women had ever been stuck with just one ghost her whole life. I was praying I wasn't going to be the first.

Not that I didn't like Frank. He was practically part of the family at this point. But he could be a little—

"Page!"

I slammed down my paper and gritted my teeth.

"What?" he said. "I've said it three times now."

Just to be contrary, I stood and went to refill my coffee cup. Frank loved coffee almost as much as he loved cigarettes. So partly I wanted more coffee and partly I just wanted to annoy him.

"Seriously?" he said, tapping phantom fingers on the kitchen table. "You're such a little kid sometimes."

"And you're more than a little dead." I refilled my coffee and leaned against the counter. "So guess who gets to decide when your page gets turned. Coffee?" I waved the steaming cup at him.

He fought a smile. "Now you're just being mean."

I heard a tap at the door and figured it was old Mrs. Lamberti from across the street. She was a friend of my nan's and would usually come by on Saturday mornings. I went to the door and opened it just as she was raising her hand to knock again.

"Morning, Mrs. L! Nan's not here—she went to the farmers' market with my mom—but you're welcome to come in for a cup of coffee if you want. She'll probably be back pretty soon."

Mrs. Lamberti went a little pink in the cheeks. "Well, you might be able to help me, Lindsay."

All my friends called me Linx, but my grandmother's friends watched me grow up as a Lindsay, and it seemed rude to correct an eighty-two-year-old woman. "Sure, what's up? Did you need help moving something?"

I'm about five foot two inches and one hundred and thirty pounds soaking wet, but Mrs. Lamberti was even smaller than me. Plus I was strong. I'd climbed plenty of walls and fences when I was a teenager, and I was pretty fit from hauling ladders and paint buckets around.

"Well…" The pink was still there. "It's not moving something. But I know Peggy says you take after her with the… other things." She crossed herself quickly, and I realized she was talking about the "ghost thing."

"Ah," I said. "Gotcha."

My grandmother and my mom didn't make a secret of the fact they saw ghosts; most people just thought they were nuts. But Venice Beach used to be pretty forgiving to eccentrics. These days, not so much. But then, nobody was going to say anything to my nan. My grandmother had lived in this neighborhood longer than anyone except Mrs. Lamberti.

"Why don't you come in for coffee?" I held the door open and ushered her to the kitchen. "Tell me what's up. I might be able to help."

"Well, it was the strangest thing," she started. "You know my hip bothers me in the mornings, so I usually don't go down to the water until it warms up."

"Uh-huh."

Frank raised an eyebrow when we walked in, any irritation with me long forgotten. He lived for this stuff. He'd been a homicide detective when he was alive. He was constantly dragging me into awkward situations that could get me arrested because they were none of my business. He regularly ignored my objections about that fact. Having something weird show up on our doorstep was probably his version of Christmas.

"So you don't go down to the water in the morning because of your hip," I prompted. "But did you do something different today?"

She sipped the cup of coffee I'd put in front of her. She took it black like my nan. "I did. I just felt like I needed to walk out on the back deck this morning. The idea just wouldn't leave me alone."

Frank stood up. "She's got a ghost. Let's go."

"Will you just calm down?" I said. "Let her talk."

Mrs. Lamberti looked around in alarm. "I'm sorry?"

I waved a hand. "That was just Frank. Go on. So you went out to the back deck?"

Mrs. Lamberti's place was a gorgeous wood-shingled house, and it sat on a quiet corner of the Sherman Canal. It was easily worth a few million dollars these days, but she'd lived there for over fifty years. Mr. Lamberti had been a builder, and he'd set his family up well.

Mrs. Lamberti was still looking around the kitchen with wide eyes, but she continued. "I went out on the back deck and noticed the plants needed watering."

"Okay...?"

"And when I went down to get the hose, I saw that

little boat my grandson keeps on our dock. You know the one?"

"Yep." I couldn't figure out where this was going. I refilled my coffee cup and sat down, prepared to settle in for a nice long ramble with Mrs. L.

"So there was the boat that Camden keeps," she continued, "and it was fine… But there was a dead man in it, so that's what I wanted to talk to you about."

I spit coffee all over the newspaper.

"Hot damn," Frank said. "This weekend just got a lot more interesting."

———

"Why aren't we calling the police again?" I asked as I walked Mrs. Lamberti back to her house, Frank trailing behind me.

"What's that, dear?"

"Nothing, Mrs. L. Let me just get you settled in the kitchen, and I'll take a look in the backyard to see if I can get anything." I glared at Frank. "And then we are definitely calling the police."

"I just want to be sure there isn't anything… odd on the back deck. You understand?"

"Of course."

If the victim had a violent death, it was very likely he'd be hanging around. I'd be able to sense him, but I wouldn't be able to see or talk to him. I could only see and talk to Frank. I'd already called my nan. This kind of stuff was her department.

"We need to take a look at the scene before the police

come," Frank said. "Once they're in, it'll be harder to get information. I need to see the body."

"No, you do not," I hissed. "If this guy was murdered—"

"Oh, I don't think it was anything like that," Mrs. Lamberti said. "I didn't see any blood. I think he was one of those sad young people with the drugs."

"Well, we'll check it out anyway."

Frank looked deflated. Drug overdose wasn't nearly as exciting as murder. "It could still be murder."

"The fact that you're hoping it was murder should be disturbing to you, Frank."

Mrs. Lamberti was used to Maxwell women talking to people she couldn't see. Luckily, modern technology had come through for mediums. I grabbed the Bluetooth earpiece for my phone and stuck it in my ear. That way if I was yelling into thin air, people would just assume I was rude, not crazy.

I crossed the street and opened Mrs. Lamberti's side door—she'd left it unlocked, of course—and started to make coffee. Frank was practically bouncing around the room he was so impatient. But I got the old woman settled with the coffeepot going before I walked toward the french doors leading out to the enormous back deck.

I took a deep breath and walked outside, prepared to feel the itch that told me a spirit was hanging around, but all I felt was Bogie.

"Hey, kid, come over here." He was already standing at the edge of the dock, looking down into the water. "Mrs. L is probably right." He sounded disappointed. "Looks like an overdose."

I wrinkled my nose. "So do I have to come and look?"

"Just get over here, Linx. It's not that bad."

I walked to the edge of the deck and looked down. Sure enough, a young Caucasian man was lying in the bottom of the red rowboat Mrs. Lamberti's grandson used on the canals. The victim had brown hair, and his eyes were closed. His mouth gaped open and his lips were a little blue. He was definitely dead. His skin was pale, and a scatter of freckles stood out on his nose. Something about the freckles made me ridiculously sad.

The boat was deep, so it didn't surprise me no one else had spotted the body. It was early enough that pedestrian traffic hadn't really started up, and few neighbors could have seen the body from their back decks, even if they'd been looking.

"You know…" I cocked my head, looking at the dead guy who was sprawled at an angle. "He doesn't look like an addict."

"Addicts look like everyone, kid."

"You know what I mean." Venice Beach had a lot of homeless people, and drugs were a problem. It wasn't uncommon to find drug paraphernalia on the street. My nan had tried to help several "wanderer friends" over the years with mixed results. My mom claimed that many of the homeless had spirits hanging around them, which was rarely a good thing.

But this guy… didn't look homeless. His clothes were clean. His hair was trimmed. "He looks more like a tech guy than a junkie." Except he had a needle in his arm. That much was pretty obvious.

Frank dissolved and reappeared in the boat next to the

body. He couldn't move anything unless he was really, really agitated, but he bent down for a closer look. "He's been here for a few hours," he said. "I'm seeing some bruising on his neck. Fingers maybe?"

"Was he choked?"

"Will you get down here?" he asked. "I can't lift his shirt, and I'm betting there are——"

"Fingerprints. Physical evidence. DNA maybe?" I crossed my arms. "None of which are mine and none of which are going to be mine, Bogie. I'm not touching that body."

"If someone held him down and put the needle in his arm, this is a murder."

"I agree. But you know who's going to have to figure that out? The police. Who we are calling right now." I pulled out my phone. "I don't feel any spirits around here, so——"

"Oh my god," said a voice beside me. "If my mother thinks I overdosed on drugs, she's going to flip out."

I turned with wide eyes to see the dead guy standing on the dock next to me.

And then *I* flipped out.

———

Mrs. Lamberti's neighbors bought my explanation for the scream because I called the police and reported the body right after they came running out to their decks. I wasn't screaming about the dead body though. It was the ghost who was sitting next to me on the bench. The ghost whom I could see clear as day. The ghost who was not Bogie.

"Will you calm down?" Frank said. "You're acting like you've never seen a spirit before."

"I see you, Frank. That's it. That's all I see. Why the hell am I seeing this guy?"

The neighbors were looking at my one-sided conversation, so I held my cell phone even as I dropped my voice.

"I'm dead," the ghost kept saying over and over again. "I can't believe I'm dead."

Frank asked, "What do you remember?"

The young man turned to Frank, narrowed his eyes. "You're a cop, aren't you?"

Frank smiled. "And you're a crook."

"What?" I asked. "Why is he a crook?"

"Because only a crook makes a cop that fast. What's your game, kid?"

He hesitated, then said, "I'm a thief. Small stuff. Nothing violent. And I don't remember what happened."

I asked Frank, "Can you really see him? I thought you said other spirits came through with static."

"They usually do." He looked pleased. "I think I can see him and talk to him better because you can see him too."

I put a hand over my face. "This is awful."

"What?" Frank asked. "Why? This is great!"

"No, it is not," I hissed under my breath. "What if he gets stuck to me too? I've already got one of you. I don't want another one."

"Hey," the dead guy said. "I'm not that bad. And I don't do drugs. Can someone tell my mom that, because she's gonna freak out."

I said, "Dude. You're dead. She's going to freak out

anyway."

He sighed and his shoulders slumped. "Shit. I can't believe I'm really dead. This is not what I was expecting death to be like."

"Did you ever really think about it?" I asked him.

"Nah." He looked guilty.

"Maybe you can just tell us who killed you," I said. "Then we can… help you to the light or something."

His eyes went wide. "There's a light?"

"There's not always a light," Frank said.

"Well, there ought to be!" I stood and paced the deck. "When is Nan getting here?"

"Miss Maxwell?" A voice spoke from the french doors. "Are you Lindsay Maxwell?"

I turned to see a nicely dressed Asian man walking toward me. He was wearing a serious expression and a suit even though the forecast said it'd be close to eighty-five degrees this afternoon.

"Cop." Frank and the dead guy both spoke at the same time.

If he was a cop, he was the best-looking one I'd run across. And unfortunately, I'd met more than my share because of Frank.

"Are you Lindsay Maxwell?" the probably-a-cop said. "I'm Detective Lee." He held out a card and I took it.

Why did Frank always have to be right?

———

A Bogie in the Boat is now available at all major retailers in e-book and paperback edition.

About the Author

ELIZABETH HUNTER is a *USA Today* and international best-selling author of romance, contemporary fantasy, and paranormal mystery. Based in Central California, she travels extensively to write fantasy fiction exploring world mythologies, history, and the universal bonds of love, friendship, and family. She has published over thirty works of fiction and sold over a million books worldwide. She is the author of Love Stories on 7th and Main, the Elemental Legacy series, the Irin Chronicles, the Cambio Springs Mysteries, and other works of fiction.

Also by Elizabeth Hunter

Contemporary Romance

The Genius and the Muse

7th and Main

INK

HOOKED (Winter 2019)

Linx & Bogie

A Ghost in the Glamour

A Bogie in the Boat

The Cambio Springs Series

Long Ride Home (short story)

Shifting Dreams

Five Mornings (short story)

Desert Bound

Waking Hearts

The Irin Chronicles

The Scribe

The Singer

The Secret

The Staff and the Blade

The Silent

The Storm

The Seeker (Fall 2018)

<u>The Elemental Mysteries</u>

A Hidden Fire

This Same Earth

The Force of Wind

A Fall of Water

<u>The Elemental World</u>

Building From Ashes

Waterlocked (novella)

Blood and Sand

The Bronze Blade (novella)

The Scarlet Deep

Beneath a Waning Moon (novella)

A Stone-Kissed Sea

<u>The Elemental Legacy</u>

Shadows and Gold

Imitation and Alchemy

Omens and Artifacts

Midnight Labyrinth

Blood Apprentice (Winter 2018)